J. T. EDSON'S
FLOATING OUTFIT

The toughest bunch of Rebels that ever lost a war, they fought for the South, and then for Texas, as the legendary Floating Outfit of "Ole Devil" Hardin's O.D. Connected ranch.

MARK COUNTER was the best-dressed man in the West: always dressed fit-to-kill. **BELLE BOYD** was as deadly as she was beautiful, with a "Manhattan" model Colt tucked under her long skirts. **THE YSABEL KID** was Comanche fast and Texas tough. And the most famous of them all was **DUSTY FOG**, the ex-cavalryman known as the Rio Hondo Gun Wizard.

J. T. Edson has captured all the excitement and adventure of the raw frontier in this magnificent Western series. Turn the page for a complete list of Berkley Floating Outfit titles.

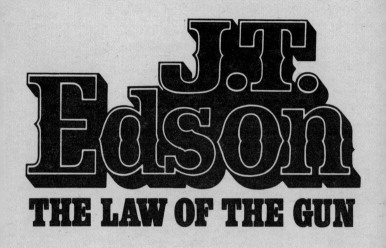

J.T. Edson

THE LAW OF THE GUN

B

BERKLEY BOOKS, NEW YORK

Originally published in Great Britain by Brown Watson Ltd.

This Berkley book contains the complete
text of the original edition.
It has been completely reset in a typeface
designed for easy reading, and was printed
from new film.

THE LAW OF THE GUN

A Berkley Book / published by arrangement with
Transworld Publishers, Ltd.

PRINTING HISTORY
Corgi edition published 1968
Berkley edition / March 1982
Second printing / June 1984

ISBN: 0-425-06840-4

A BERKLEY BOOK ® TM 757,375
Berkley Books are published by The Berkley Publishing Group,
200 Madison Avenue, New York, New York 10016.
The name "BERKLEY" and the stylized "B" with design
are trademarks belonging to Berkley Publishing Corporation.
PRINTED IN THE UNITED STATES OF AMERICA

For Myrtle Molloy,
the wild colonial girl.

THE LAW OF THE GUN

CHAPTER ONE

Ballinger's Plan

"You're crazy, Ed," stated Captain Francis Mulrooney. "If you're caught at it, nothing can save you."

The tall, powerful, craggy-faced man seated at the other side of Mulrooney's desk grinned, showing his prominent teeth. Perched on his head at a rakish angle, the curly-brimmed derby hat pressed down his bay-rum scented hair. He wore a suit of the latest style, though not of expensive material, white shirt and neatly-fastened tie. A lead-loaded, plaited leather billy sagged down his jacket's outer right pocket. Inside his breast pocket lay a leather wallet holding a gold and silver police lieutenant's badge and a card identifying Edward Frank Ballinger as a member of the Chicago Police Department's newly-formed Detective Bureau.

"It's likely to be the only chance we'll ever have of laying the arm on Tony Reckharts, Cis," Ballinger replied. "Everybody in the Blue Boar'll be so busy watching Gallus Maggie and Sadie the Goat that I could walk up and snatch the till off the bar without them noticing me."

Slowly Mulrooney crushed out the glowing end of the cigar he held, then studied the face of his most able subordinate. The bulky Chief of Detectives had brains as well as brawn and was also honest; something which did not necessarily follow with his position. Being honest, he hated criminals, especially those of Reck-

1

harts' breed. Not, Mulrooney frankly admitted, that one could find many criminals with Reckharts' brilliance, knowledge of the law and organizing ability. In fact, Reckharts stood alone in Chicago's underworld – for which the Windy City might count itself very fortunate. While arresting Reckharts would deal a crushing, if not final, blow to organized crime in the city, Mulrooney did not wish to achieve it at the cost of Ballinger's life.

If the scheme which Ballinger had just put forward worked – although armchair moralists might question its legality – the evidence he gathered would put Reckharts away for a long time – even if they could not put a permanent end to his menace by hanging him. Should the plan go wrong in any detail, Ballinger faced a stiff jail sentence – or more likely a painful death and a watery grave in the depths of Lake Michigan. Knowing something of Reckharts, Mulrooney expected the latter alternative, for dead men tell no tales.

"You know what it'll mean if you get caught?" Mulrooney asked, and when Ballinger nodded, went on: "Then you're dead set on going through with it?"

"Sure. I'm sick to my guts of seeing Reckharts and his top men running the law ragged and laughing in our faces every time we haul one of them into court."

"Reckon you can trust the Yegg?"

"He's a good guy, apart from his habit of busting open safes," Ballinger replied. "And his family means a lot to him. Reckharts met his sister, she was a good-looking gal—"

"Was?" asked Mulrooney.

"That body we fished out of the lake, the one with no face left," said Ballinger quietly. "The Yegg identified it as his sister. She was four months pregnant – and the family hadn't seen her since Reckharts took her to his place in Streeterville. Yeah. I reckon I can trust the Yegg."

"Then the only way I can stop you going through

with this's to put you in jail,'' growled Mulrooney. "You know my position, Ed. Officially I don't know a thing about this. Unofficially, good luck and I hope you pull it off. Of course, it all depends on whether Maggie and Sadie tangle.''

"They'll do that all right," Ballinger promised.

All the Badlands, that sprawling area of slums surrounding the stockyards, bubbled with excitement and conjecture. On every street, in every saloon, honky-tonk, dance hall, billiards parlor and brothel only one topic received discussion. A stranger seeking accommodation in the gambling line would have found but one subject on which the citizens of the Badlands wished to stake their wealth: if Gallus Maggie Drayton and Sadie 'the Goat' Barkis tangled, what would be the outcome?

When two ladies each seek and aspire to the highest social position in any society, a clash can always be expected. The nature of the clash depends upon what strata of society the ladies grace. As Sadie the Goat and Gallus Maggie each claimed pre-eminence in the city's lusty, brawling underworld, their clash might be expected to pass beyond the verbal stage and offer its witnesses quite a spectacle. Gallus Maggie, so called because she occasionally donned men's clothing and supported the pants with suspenders – known as galluses among her numerous admirers – was the belle of the Pine Road Rollers, and ran a saloon with a reputation for toughness only equalled by Sadie the Goat's establishment, which served as headquarters for the East Stockyard Boys.

Possibly their feud might never have gone beyond the stage of discredit name-calling and boasting, had not romance reared its head. Each lady was aware that the outcome of a clash would be anything but certain and might have stayed content to utter threats and claim a moral victory when the other failed to take up the challenge.

Then Reckharts came along. In his capacity as organizer of crime, he made use of members from the Rollers and the Boys. While visiting the respective hangouts of the gangs, he made the acquaintance of Maggie and Sadie. Being a man with an eye for the ladies, and an insatiable desire to make conquests of the opposite sex, he wooed and won both – dwelling in the fond belief that neither knew of his relationship with the other. Reckharts knew the fury of a woman scorned, and wanted no trouble with Maggie or Sadie. So he tried to keep his affairs a secret.

Somehow word leaked out. Just how much a certain detective-lieutenant knew about the leak was never established. It *could* have been pure coincidence that Ed Ballinger visited each gang's hang-out on the night before the rumors became public knowledge.

Even then the women might have ignored the issue, but word reached Maggie that Sadie openly claimed to have sole right of entry to Reckharts' Blue Boar Saloon, and that no galluses-wearing cow had best show her face inside. Curiously, at the same time that Maggie heard of Saddie's threat, Miss Barkis received warning that if she entered the Blue Boar, Miss Drayton intended to see that she did not walk out.

Such a direct challenge could not be ignored on either side. Each gang's power in its district rested too much on the fear it inspired and, in no small measure, to certain talents displayed by its most prominent female member. Each girl acted as senior bouncer in her saloon, differing only in their mode of evicting a trouble-maker. Gallus Maggie perfected a trick by which she felled the awkward one, then pounced on him, or her, gripped the offender's ear in her teeth and dragged him to the door. If the offender gave further trouble, and sometimes even if he, or she, did not, Maggie would continue biting until she severed the ear from its roots. Behind her bar, kept pickled for posterity, stood no less than ten ears. While not going in for such elaborate trophies, Sadie also used her own technique for dealing with the obstreperous. Lowering her head, she charged at the annoying party like an old billy goat, thereby gaining her name, to deliver a butt to the body which laid her victim in a winded and unresisting heap upon the floor. After that Sadie took whatever further action she considered necessary.

From which it could be seen that a clash between two such talented temperaments had great spectator-interest and value.

Ed Ballinger had been born and raised in Chicago, knowing the sprawling city like the back of his hand. Very little happened that, sooner or later, he did not hear about and he had been aware of the smouldering feud between the two ladies. At first he ignored the matter, having more important business to occupy him. Then he saw the possibilities of the situation if properly handled. Ordinary legal methods would never lay Reckharts low, he covered his tracks too well for that. A chance meeting put Ballinger in the way of gaining evidence which would not only bring Reckharts into his hands, but smash the man's vast criminal empire too.

In a way if had been Reckharts' insatiable lust for women which gave Ballinger his chance. Having his finger in almost every criminal pie in a five hundred square miles area, Reckharts' ego desired he be called 'Big Man' by his underlings. One of them, known as the Yegg, specialized in opening locked safes and other such depositories of wealth. An intelligent man, the Yegg served an apprenticeship in a legitimate firm of locksmiths and safe makers. In the early 1870's he stood at the height of his new, if illegal, profession and brought 'peter-popping' to a fine art. Being known as a 'straight' man who would never talk if arrested, he found much employment in projects organized by the Big Man; Reckharts paid well, planned and arranged each job so that little could go wrong, and the Yegg might have continued working indefinitely—had he not had a pretty young sister.

Despite entanglements with at least two other ladies, neither of whom would have approved, Reckharts came, saw and conquered the Yegg's sister. Unfortunately he loved not wisely, but too well. The Yegg's sister proved to have a strongly independent streak and refused to be patted on the head, presented with money and quietly shunted off into oblivion. It transpired that she had brains as well as beauty, although her selection of male company might have argued against such a possession. She knew enough about Reckharts' activities to make casting her aside alive and able to talk decidedly risky, and continued to press her demands for a matrimonial settlement.

A wise general, Reckharts never ordered a major assault while support for the opposition hovered on his flank. Knowing the strong family ties between the Yegg and his sister, the Big Man planned accordingly. After sending the Yegg instructions to pop a safe in a business building, Reckharts passed word to a police officer, who augmented his civic salary with donations from the Big Man and gave much useful service in return, giving certain orders.

At which point Reckharts' plan started to go wrong. While not claiming to be a genius, Ed Ballinger could add two and two with some accuracy. When he saw a police officer dressing in the latest fashions, living in an apartment the rental of which would be equal to almost his full salary, eating at the best places and tossing money around, Ballinger became suspicious. The lieutenant probed to some effect, learning enough to ensure the errant officer's arrest and dismissal. In order to avoid any scandal against the department, Ballinger handled the matter himself and in private. While tying up the loose ends, even though they could not take him to Reckharts, he, and not the man to which it had been intended, received the instructions for the Yegg's disposal. Time being short, Ballinger made the arrest instead of assigning it to one of his subordinates. At the back of his mind lurked the possibility that the Yegg might turn informer, given certain facts.

The Yegg accepted his arrest with a fatalistic attitude, regarding it as no more than the law of averages turning against him. Even hearing that the arresting officer had been under orders to either kill or seriously injure him during the apprehension did not change his mind; for he regarded the news as being a police trick.

Pure chance stepped in at that point. Taking the Yegg to headquarters, Ballinger decided to keep the arrest a secret for a time. So he escorted his man through the rear of the building, arriving just as a horse-drawn ambulance brought in a body found in Lake Michigan. The features had been obliterated by vitriol or another corrosive agent, but the Yegg identified the body as his sister, recognizing a birthmark on the shoulder and a scar on the thigh. Chance alone let him see the first mark, glancing with morbid interest as Ballinger drew back the sheet covering the body to look at it. There had been no chance in the second identifying mark, for the Yegg insisted on making sure – or trying to convince himself that the ruined thing before him was not his sister.

From the moment of discovery, the Yegg wanted only one thing: his revenge on the man responsible for her death. Even in his grief, he could think and knew that he could accomplish nothing alone against Reckharts for the Big Man stood behind a barrier of hired toughs. So the Yegg agreed to help Ballinger in every way he could.

Among other things the Yegg told Ballinger, he mentioned Reckharts' safe and that it contained enough evidence to hang the Big Man and smash his organization. The only fly in that ointment being how to gain access to the safe's contents. Asking for a search warrant might have struck some people as the obvious

answer to the problem, but in law enforcement the obvious only rarely provided the right answer. Reckharts
had never been *proven* the brains behind much of
Chicago's crime and his wealth gave him some considerable social standing with friends in high places.
Should Ballinger apply for the warrant, there would be
delay in obtaining it. During that delay word would
reach Reckharts and allow him to destroy, or hide away,
all the incriminating evidence.

The Yegg claimed he could, given the opportunity,
open the safe one-handed and left-handed at that. One
very important detail prevented him from doing so; the
safe reposed in Reckharts' *very* private office on the
floor above his Blue Boar Saloon's bar-room. Knowing
the value of the safe's contents, Reckharts took precautions against the wrong people gaining access to it.

Discarding the idea of gaining legal possession of the
safe's contents, Ballinger gave thought to arranging an
opportunity for the Yegg to exercise his talents. The
smouldering feud between Gallus Maggie and Sadie the
Goat presented Ballinger with the basis of that opportunity. Having seen victims of each woman's evic-
tion methods, Ballinger did not hesitate to set them at
each other's throats. Nobody, not even those who had
lost an ear to Maggie or had had hair torn from the
scalp by Sadie, ever dared take the matter before a
judge, which made any attempt at convicting and
punishing the women impossible. The way Ballinger saw
it, such damage as Maggie and Sadie inflicted upon each
other would be in payment for the treatment they had
handed to others. Ed Ballinger was neither an armchair
moralist, nor a dreamy-eyed liberal-intellectual; so, free
from the disinterested bigotry of either, his thinking
bore the mark of good, sound common sense.

Only Ballinger knew that he caught the Yegg in the
act of breaking a safe. In fact nobody at headquarters
even knew that the Yegg had been there on that fateful
night; the two men of the ambulance crew did not

belong to the Police Department and knew nothing of the Yegg's criminal past, believing him to be a relative brought in to identify the body.

Being released, the Yegg acted as he would under normal conditions in the circumstances. He went into hiding and passed word through the usual channels informing Reckharts that the job had gone sour, although he escaped arrest. To add authenticity to the message, the Yegg requested that his sister be informed not to worry and requested speedy re-employment.

Maybe Reckharts would have gone much deeper into the matter, but he found himself with some highly diverting trouble on his hands. His information service at headquarters notified him of the arrest of his man, which accounted for the Yegg's continued freedom. Reckharts gave no thought to the arrested policeman. On several occasions the Big Man had warned about spending beyond one's legal earnings, but the fool did not listen. So he had made a slip and Ballinger slammed home the jaws of a trap. Reckharts did not care, knowing that the dishonest lawman could in no way implicate him. While the loss had spoiled one plan, Reckharts could rely on other police contacts. The Yegg apparently had not heard of his sister's death, and might not. If he did, he could be removed later in the manner planned.

The news which diverted Reckharts was that Sadie the Goat intended to be in his place at noon on Saturday and that Gallus Maggie had expressed her expectancy of being present also. Such a meeting could have only one result. While Reckharts' ego received quite a boost at the thought of two women fighting for his affections, he wished they could have found some other venue for the fracas. Unfortunately for him, Maggie heard that Sadie would be visiting his place and realized that such an action threw down the gauntlet which she must take up. Curiously, at the time Maggie heard of her rival's intentions, Sadie was receiving word that Maggie meant to

be at the Blue Boar on Saturday at noon in defiance of
Sadie's warning. Possibly each woman felt some
trepidation as she heard the fateful words. Yet each
knew she must be at Reckharts' place on Saturday at
noon – or get out of Chicago. Too much attention had
been attracted to their comments and word of the
challenge spread like the wind-blown flames of a prairie
fire. Speculation as to the result rose high and each
woman knew she could not avoid the issue.

Sensing the danger posed by the clash, Reckharts
took steps to avert it. Using his influence, he called in
senior members of the Pine Road Rollers and the East
Stockyard Boys. Both outfits' representatives knew that
Reckharts possessed sufficient evidence to get all
present hanged, or jailed for life, without danger to
himself; so they tended to be complacent and listen to
his demands. To avoid a full-scale gang battle which
might wreck the blue Boar, Reckharts stipulated rules.
Firstly, only two men and two women members of each
gang would accompany their representative to the Blue
Boar. Secondly, the rest of the gangs would remain in
their own territory and make no attempt to either attend
the fight or seek out their rivals. Being aware of
Reckharts' power to make them uncomfortable, the
delegation agreed to his rules.

Word raced around the town that the clash would
come off. Ballinger heard the news and felt his pulse
quicken. He had set the scene, assembled the cast, laid
down the basis of the plot. If his plan succeeded, he
would have all the evidence he needed to convict
Reckharts and break the Big Man's evil power. Should
the plan fail in any way – Ballinger tried to avoid
thinking of the consequences of failure.

CHAPTER TWO

Two Ladies Prepare for Conflict

A hand clapped in a familiar manner on the Yegg's shoulder as he stood among the crowd gathered before the Blue Boar Saloon on Saturday morning. No man, even with the stimulus of revenge to sustain him, planned to betray Reckharts without feeling qualms and becoming somewhat nervous. So the Yegg turned like a startled pronghorn antelope and looked up at a grimy, unshaven, heavily moustached face which seemed vaguely familiar but whose identity eluded him. A peaked uniform hat, battered and grease-encrusted; dirty, striped jersey; oil-stiffened peajacket, equally unkempt trousers and sea-boots which clad the stranger hinted that he served as an engineer on one of the Great Lakes boats. Why the man should exhibit such friendly familiarity was beyond the safe-breaker.

"You getting too high-toned to talk to an old friend, Yegg?" asked the stranger – in Ed Ballinger's voice.

The Yegg's mouth dropped open as he stared at the begrimed, unkempt figure which looked so different form the normally smart, neatly-dressed detective-lieutenant. Even with the voice, he could hardly believe that Ballinger stood at his side.

"What—!" the Yegg began. "How—?".

"Shut your mouth before you get flies in it," grinned Ballinger. "I got to figuring that Reckharts wouldn't take it kindly if he saw me going up his stairs. So I made a few changes. Think anybody'll recognize me?''

"I don't reckon your own mother would," answered the Yegg. "That moustache—"

"It's a fake," Ballinger explained. "A friend who works in the theatre fixed it for me. Grew the stubble myself though."

"Thought so," the Yegg answered, his spirits rising now he found himself alongside a man whom most criminals feared as the toughest elbow in the Windy City. "It's the only part that looks phoney."

"The bartender inside's supposed to be some light-house," the detective warned. "He might spot me."

Despite the head bartender's ability at recognizing detectives – which gave him the honorary title of "Lighthouse" – Yegg felt confident that Ballinger could enter without being identified.

"Any sign of them yet?" he asked, after displaying his confidence to Ballinger.

"Not so far. But we'd best get inside. It's likely to be crowded later."

On approaching the doors of the Blue Boar, Ballinger saw that the crowd had already begun. Almost every table appeared to be filled with customers even though a pair of big, burly bouncers stood just inside and controlled, or restricted entrance. Clearly Reckharts intended his place to be occupied only by the upper-classes for such an important event, leaving the riff-raff to stand outside and see what they could from the sidewalks. However, as a master-craftsman, the Yegg had the right of entry.

"Who's this feller?" demanded the bigger bouncer, eyeing Ballinger up and down.

"He's all right," the Yegg answered. "Engineer on a boat making the Jack Cannuck run, and a friend of mine."

Knowing the advantage of keeping on the right side of personnel who worked on boats which crossed the international border to Canadian ports, the bouncer accepted the Yegg's guarantee and stood aside allowing the two men to enter the bar.

Give him his due, Reckharts ran a fancy place. Some of the country's top entertainers had appeared on the stage at the end of the room and a good orchestra mostly occupied the railed-off pit below it. Tables and chairs, all of them occupied, covered most of the floor. The Blue Boar made its profit on drinks sold during the entertainment and did not offer gambling or private dancing. However, a large, clear space had been left before the long, mahogany bar. Curiously under the circumstances, only a few customers stood at the bar; and the numerous waiters appeared to be collecting drinks for the seated customers from a back room. Studying his surroundings, Ballinger noticed that the normal display of bottled drinks had been removed from the shelves behind the bar. While red drapes hung over the long bar mirror which was Reckharts' pride and joy, a gap in them showed that they hid a wooden shield protecting the glass. Clearly Reckharts intended to keep damage to his property to a minimum.

Despite the Yegg's confidence, Ballinger felt just a twinge of concern as the bartender noted for his "lighthouse" ability looked him over. The disguise appeared to be foolproof for the bartender nodded a jovial greeting. Knowing how his men felt about selling a fellow criminal – especially one regarded as harmless and straight – to the law, Reckharts had not mentioned his plans for the Yegg, so the bouncer and bartender showed no surprise at seeing the little safe-breaker present.

"First's on the house, gents," announced the bartender, after learning of Ballinger's supposed position in life. "Only after you've drunk it, I wouldn't stop at the bar. It's likely to get mighty unhealthy for bystanders. The boss aims to have Gallus and the Goat make their fight out here."

"Thanks, Lighthouse," the Yegg answered. "Best

give us a bottle and two glasses, then we'll find some place where we can see the fun.''

''Was I you, I'd go up the stairs and stand on the balcony. Unless you be joining the Big Man at his table.''

''We'll go upstairs. The company wouldn't suit us at the Big Man's table,'' replied the Yegg, with a sly wink as if to imply that, while a useful man in some ways, his companion was hardly the type one took into such exalted society.

''Sure,'' agreed the bartender, returning the wink. ''Tell Gimp up there I said you could pick where you want to be.''

''Thanks, Lighthouse.''

''That's all right, Yegg. You're a straight eel. Too bad that crack fell through on Tuesday.''

''There'll be others,'' the Yegg answered, taking bottle and glasses then turning to walk towards the stairs.

A frown creased the bartender's brow as he watched Ballinger follow the Yegg. There had been something familiar about that big, mean-looking cuss and he certainly did not seem to be the kind the Yegg associated with. If it had been anybody with a less straight reputation, the bartender mused – then gave a shrug. Hell, more than one man working the Great Lakes boats augmented his salary at the boss's expense. Most likely the Yegg's companion had been in the bar before, which accounted for the feeling of acquaintanceship. Any further thoughts which the bartender might have had on the subject chopped off as customers demanded service.

The broad staircase led up to the building's second floor. At its head a wide balcony overlooked the barroom and was lined with private rooms in which numerous things could – and did – happen. Already a fair crowd of lesser social lights gathered on the balcony so as to be in position and obtain a good view of the fracas. Several of Reckharts' muscular bouncers stood at vantage points ready to quell any disturbances which arose through over-excitement or when old enemies rubbed shoulders in the crowd. Standing at the head of the stairs, twirling a pick handle with the casual nonchalance of a patrolman idling on his beat, the biggest bouncer of them all nodded a greeting to the Yegg. After giving Ballinger a careful scrutiny, the bouncer listened to the bartender's request for the Yegg to be given good accommodation. The Yegg's social standing gave him the right to a seat downstairs, the bouncer raised no objections to the request.

"Just say where you want to go, Mr. Yegg," he said.

"Top of the stairs here'll do fine, Gimp," the Yegg replied. "If those gents wouldn't mind making room."

While the "gents" probably did mind, they moved along. Nobody in his right mind argued with the head bouncer when he twirled his deadly pick handle and made a request.

Having seen his guests in a place which met with their approval, Gimp turned to move along the balcony and quell an argument rising between supporters of the two ladies.

"The office's up the passage, on the right," breathed the Yegg.

Making his movements as casual as possible, Ballinger turned and looked around as if overwhelmed by the magnificence of his surroundings. A short passage separated the side rooms and faced the head of the stairs. At the far end was a door against which a bulky bouncer leaned in a sulky manner.

"Will he be there all the time?" Ballinger asked, as he swung back to face the Yegg and reached for the bottle his companion held.

"Maybe supposed to be," answered the Yegg, doing the honors by pouring out a couple of drinks. "But I'll take money he moves forward to see the fight."

"We'll have to take him out if he doesn't," the lieutenant warned.

"That's your game. I don't go on the muscle."

"Sure. You leave him to me."

"I aim to do just that," stated the safe-breaker. "Know anybody down there, Ed?"

Looking down, Ballinger studied the various tables in the room and then nodded his head. "It looks like the jail's turned out. There're more thieves here than I've ever seen in one place before."

Practically every criminal of any prominence in Chicago and the neighboring cities sat in the room, rubbing shoulders with a number of influential citizens one would have thought ought not to be in such company. Ballinger grinned coldly as he thought how many of the men in the room would be disappearing behind bars if the Yegg opened Reckharts' safe and it proved to be the cornucopia the peterman promised.

Thinking of that caused Ballinger to seek out and look over the Big Man. Not that finding Reckharts proved any problem. Although situated at the rear of the room, Reckharts' table had a wide, clear avenue stretching before it and allowing its occupants a clear view of the battle area. Seated around the table, including a prominent judge whom Ballinger promised a bad end, were the élite of criminal Chicago and the Big Man himself.

When he looked at Reckharts, Ballinger wondered if he would ever understand female mentality, for he was at a loss to explain the Big Man's fascination to the opposite sex. Certainly it could not be attributed to handsome features. Reckharts' face had a complexion like freshly-stirred river mud, piggy black eyes, a nose two sizes too large and a small, thin-lipped mouth. Nor did he possess the kind of physique which made women's mouths water, although his tailor did the best possible with a slightly over middle height, dumpy frame. An expensive grey suit of the latest style and cut sat unhappily on Reckharts' body and a diamond almost the size of a pigeon's egg decorated the stickpin in his cravat. Pudgy fingers on one hand toyed with a cigar almost as long and thick as a patrolman's night-stick, while the other hand held a comb with which he emphasized whatever point of conversation he made, or passed through his bay-rum slicked, middle-parted hair.

Wondering what the hell women saw in Reckharts, Ballinger turned his attention to the man seated at the mastermind's right side. Tall, lean, dressed in a stylish city suit, although not looking either comfortable or happy in it, the man at Reckharts' right hand did not have the appearance of a city dweller. Few people in a city ever achieved such a tanned appearance and the man's cheeks looked to have been assaulted by the elements until they had turned to the color of old saddle leather. Although Ballinger searched into the back of his mind, he could not put a name to the lean man's face.

Nor could the Yegg when Ballinger placed the problem to him.

"Never seen him before," the safe-breaker answered. "But he's sure somebody to be sat there. Mugs O'Toole usually has that seat."

"Yeah," agreed Ballinger. "Only I don't see Mugs around."

The Yegg had also found Reckharts' chief bodyguard conspicuous by his absence and been on the point of mentioning the fact. Normally the big, brutal O'Toole could be found at Reckharts' right side and it hardly seemed likely he would be absent at a time when so many potential rivals were present.

Before either Ballinger or the Yegg could discuss the matter further, a low rumble of talk welled up and every eye turned to the main doors. A small party, three women and two men, entered and walked towards the bar. The men wore flashy suits and were clearly aware of their position as the centre of attraction. Two of the women sported large brimmed hats and garish gowns which spelled class and fashion in the Badlands.

While much bejewelled, the third woman wore simpler clothes. Her sleeveless white blouse clung to her rich, full bust in a manner which showed that she dispensed with any garment beneath it and the plain black skirt could not hide the splendid hips and power- ful legs underneath. Five-foot-ten she stood, a blonde Juno with reasonably good features and a figure which met with the crowd's approval. Thirty-five years of rough life had still not destroyed Gallus Maggie's looks or shape; she looked fit, healthy and as strong as a dockside roustabout. On reaching the bar, she set a glass jar full of pickling fluid upon the shining surface, waved a hand to Reckharts and bought her supporters a round of drinks.

From the street came an excited buzz of conversation, the kind of noise one heard at a prize-fight when the challenger came into sight and approached the ring.

"Here's Sadie," the Yegg breathed.

Sadie the Goat in no way looked like one of her namesake. Although slightly shorter and lighter than Maggie, she still was a tolerable hunk of woman. Black hair, cut short so as to avoid any cushioning of the im- pact when performing her famous head butt, framed an almost beautiful face. Despite being involved in more than one female fracas, Sadie retained her good looks. She wore much the same style clothes as Maggie, her skirt striped and a blouse of even more daring cut. Size and weight might favor Gallus Maggie, but Sadie had speed and, at twenty-two, the advantage of youth. Jewelry exceeding even Maggie's display glinted about Sadie as she and her escort went to the other end of the bar.

Immediately the few customers who stood at the bar moved and after sliding drinks to Sadie's party, the bar- tender slipped out of what could be a danger area to make his way to the place he had picked out as his van- tage point for the forthcoming hostilities.

"Go tell that short-haired cow to get out and stop

stinking up the joint,'' Maggie requested.

"Ask that fat old whore if she thinks she could put me out,'' Sadie called back even before the message could be relayed.

Clearly neither intended to rush headlong into the conflict. After the preliminary insults, each woman's quartet of supporters gathered around their principal and went into a muttered discussion. Silence fell on the room and if Ballinger had felt any doubts about the plan succeeding, they began to ebb away. Everybody's attention, with the exception of the detective and the Yegg, was fixed upon the two groups at the bar and stayed there oblivious of the surrounding company.

"Now?'' breathed the Yegg.

"Let them start fighting first,'' Ballinger answered, glancing back and seeing the bouncer still at his post. From the way the man craned his neck and raised himself on tip-toe in an attempt to see what happened in the bar-room, he would be unlikely to resist temptation once the fracas began.

Turning from his party, the leader of the Pine Road Rollers advanced half-way along the bar. Showing just as much care to appear casual and inoffensive, the head of the East Stockyard Boys moved to meet his opposite number.

"Sadie says she'll fight barefoot if Maggie does,'' announced the leader of the Boys.

"So be it,'' agreed the boss of the Rollers.'' Only our gals search the Goat.''

Both precautions proved to have some merit, although it could not be said that either participant was blameless of trying to gain an advantage. While Maggie happened to be wearing a pair of steel-toed men's boots – purely in the interest of setting a new fashion – a check on Sadie's more formal footwear revealed that each sole had a razor-edged knife blade stitched into it. A search of Sadie produced a set of knuckledusters slipped into the bosom of her blouse, but the finding of a push-knife sheathed to Maggie's garter nullified any protest she might have made.

Standing at the bar after being thoroughly searched, Maggie glanced at her hands. The heavy rings she wore would rip Sadie's face to ribbons, but the Goat's fingers carried no less impressive an armoury. Slowly Maggie reached up and removed her earrings.

"Tell her to put all her jewelery in a hat, and I'll drop mine in," she declared. "Winner, which'll be me, gets it all."

No more eager to be on the receiving end of blows backed with the bulky stones of her opponent's rings, Sadie agreed.

"I don't know what I'll do with a pile of glass and trash like she's wearing, but I'll go along with her."

A signal to the bartender brought him forward. In passing he borrowed a customer's hat and into it deposited some thousand dollars' worth of jewelry – at fence's prices for none of it could have been offered on the legitimate market without considerable danger of arrest. Turning, the bartender took a hurried departure; an example followed by each girl's representatives.

"It's starting!"

The mumble, audible through repetition, went around the crowd which blocked the street and crowded the sidewalk. A solid wall of faces almost shut out the daylight from the windows and heads peered both over and under the batwing doors. Inside the bar, a pin falling to the floor might have been heard. Probably the point of that same pin could have been thrust into the flesh of any of the onlookers without them feeling it.

Despite his interest in the affair which brought him to the Blue Boar, Ballinger found his mouth had gone dry while watching the two women being searched. He ran the tip of his tongue across his lips. At his side, the Yegg breathed heavily and kept his eyes fixed on Reckharts' face. Only by doing so could the safe-breaker remember his mission of revenge.

Sadie turned for the first time to look at Maggie. Slowly the blonde swung around and faced her black-haired rival.

"You know what I said about you coming here?" Maggie asked, hoping her voice sounded normal. "Now get out or I'll pickle your ear."

"Any time you're ready to try it, you old tub of lard," Sadie answered, trying to sound calmer and more assured than she felt, "just make a start and try."

Bare feet slapping down on the floor and sounding loud in the silence, the two queens of the Chicago underworld moved warily towards each other.

CHAPTER THREE

Two Ladies and a Gentleman
Each Acquire Trophies

Suddenly Maggie made the opening move. Knotting her left hand into a fist, she threw a blow in the direction of Sadie's face. Driven by an arm with muscles that a strong man might not have felt ashamed to possess, the fist packed enough power to knock Sadie flat; only to do so it had to connect. Having some experience in fistic matters, Sadie knew the dangers of the situation and planned accordingly. Fast as a cat, she side-stepped and Maggie's big fist scraped her hair in passing. The force of the blow and the surprise of it missing threw Maggie off balance. Around and forward whipped Sadie's left fist, slamming hard into the blonde's belly. Air exploded in a gasp of agony from Maggie's lips. Her body hunched in pain and she reeled back until her shoulders struck the bar. Looking winded and dazed, Maggie hung on the polished mahogany, wide open for whatever came next.

Down went Sadie's head and those who had been privileged to witness her in action before tensed in expectation. A low moan of sympathy rose from that section of the crowd who had a financial interest in Maggie's success as Sadie launched herself forward in the start of the devastating move which gave her her name. On every other occasion when Sadie had dealt a woman such a blow, the recipient had been all but done even without the charge that ended with a hard head smashing into the belly or bust. Confidently she hurtled forward, preparing to hand Maggie a *coup de grâce*.

But Sadie made a mistake. This time the woman on whom she launched her "goat butt" was harder and tougher than any other the black-haired girl had ever met. Winded and hurt Maggie might have been by the unexpected blow, but her body could take punishment and her dazed appearance was more assumed than actual. As Sadie approached, with head lowered and body bent forward, Maggie timed the move and drove up her right knee. Luck favored Sadie. Instead of taking Maggie's rising knee in the centre of her face, she caught the impact on her forehead. The force halted Sadie's attempted butt, lifted her erect and sent her staggering.

A howl of disappointment and anguish rose from Sadie's supporters as she lost her balance and fell flat on her back. Echoing the sympathy came a delighted yell from the Maggie fanciers as the big blonde hurled herself forward, landed on Sadie and lowered her head, with the mouth open for a bite. Jerking her head aside, Sadie heard the click of Maggie's teeth closing alongside her ear. Down jerked the black head, against the side of Maggie's neck. The blonde's body gave a convulsive jerk and a scream burst from her lips as Sadie's teeth sank into the soft flesh where her neck curved out to form her shoulder. Digging her fingers into Sadie's hair, Maggie tried to tear the other's teeth from their grasp. Agony drove through Maggie and her fingers sent burning fires knifing into Sadie's scalp, but the teeth still held firm, gripping and tearing. Maggie threw herself from the lighter girl with such violence that Sadie, still biting, lifted from the floor, landed on top of the blonde, then went over. Knowing the danger of fighting at close quarters with the heavier Maggie, Sadie released her hold and let herself roll across the floor. The short black hair did not lend itself to firm grasping and Maggie's fingers lost their hold as Sadie's weight went from her and the teeth released her flesh.

Sadie came to her feet, landing crouched and preparing to launch another attack. Although she hoped to make a move before the other recovered, Sadie saw that Maggie had also stood up. Blood ran in a scarlet trickle from the side of Maggie's neck, across her chest and down the valley between her breasts. Ignoring the stinging sensation which remained even though the teeth no longer gripped her flesh, Maggie stalked towards the smaller girl.

"Get at her, Maggie!" screamed a voice. "Have her ear!"

"Go for her, Sadie," countered another. "Give her the 'goat' ".

Neither woman gave any sign that she had heard her supporters' advice. The opening moves had confirmed what each woman already knew: that she faced a hard, savage struggle, one fraught with danger. A wrong move, a single slip, could leave the incautious one at the other's mercy – only no mercy would be shown. With so much at stake, Sadie and Maggie did not aim to indulge in any rash chance-taking. Each had tried her pet move and seen it fail, with some pain resulting from the failure, and did not intend to try it again until a more suitable opportunity presented itself.

Out lashed Sadie's fist, cracking against Maggie's cheek, but the blonde gave no more than a grunt to show she felt the blow. Twice more the lighter girl snapped home punches, then Maggie hit back, sinking a hard punch into Sadie's body. After taking a couple more of Maggie's heavy punches, Sadie saw the danger of trying to out-slug the bigger, heavier blonde. Using the skill and knowledge gained in her rough way of life, Sadie speeded up her tactics as a method of offsetting her lack of heft. Watched by the crowd, which grew more excited by the second, Sadie jumped, ducked and sidestepped in an attempt to avoid taking Maggie's blows and ripped home punches which jolted the blonde. Her tactics partially succeeded and less than one in four of Maggie's swings connected. When the blows did connect, Sadie knew about them for Maggie had learned fighting in just as hard a school and knew how to throw a punch.

For almost two minutes it might have been two men fighting, the way fists hammered at flesh. Sweat ran down the women's faces but they did not slacken the fury of their efforts. Then Maggie caught Sadie full in the centre of the face, taking the other by surprise. Sadie let out a squeal as hard knuckles crushed her nose. Staggering back, tears of pain blinded her and blood dribbled from her nostrils. A low hiss went through the crowd as Sadie received her first bloodletting. She caught her balance and discarded fist fighting. Flinging herself forward, she drove her fingers into Maggie's hair. The moment Maggie felt the tearing at her hair, she dropped fistic tactics and became pure woman. Up rose Maggie's hands, sinking into the short black locks and this time retaining their hold. Around they spun, locked to each other, feet kicking and hooking round the other's legs.

The sight of two good-looking women locked in savage conflict had such a sensual, primeval attraction that the Yegg and Ballinger almost forgot their reason for being at the Blue Boar. Standing at the head of the stairs, surrounded by excited supporters, the Yegg happened to look across the room and beyond the fighters to where Reckharts and his party sat around the big table watching the fight with rapt attention. Reckharts' face was twisted into lines of sadistic pleasure and sweat beaded his brow as he watched the fighting women lose their balance and go crashing to the barroom floor. At which point the Yegg came out of his trance. Before his eyes rose the sight of a beautiful, happy girl, then the vision of the hideous wreck of her face.

"Ed!" he said, looking at the detective. Drawing back his elbow he thrust it hard into Ballinger's ribs. "Ed. For the Lord's sake!"

Giving a grunt of anger, Ballinger swung towards his assailant. While the detective had seen women fight before, their efforts had been mild compared with the savagery with which Maggie and Sadie tore into each other. The booze or jealousy inspired hair-pullings Ballinger had witnessed paled into nothing compared with the raw fury of these two gorgeous women.

"What the—!" Ballinger began.

"Snap out of it, Lieutenant!" the Yegg ordered.

A momentary fear hit the Yegg as he realized that he had spoken aloud. Then he saw that none of the people around had paid the slightest attention to him, having eyes and ears only for the fight. The words brought Ballinger back to a realization of who, what and where he was.

Turning from the fight, Ballinger looked back over the heads of the people behind him. As he expected, the bouncer no longer stood watch outside Reckharts' office but had moved forward and joined the crowd, exerting his superior weight to force himself through the crowd for a frontal position. Studying the bouncer's complete enthrallment, Ballinger guessed that he would be unlikely to return to his post as long as the fight lasted.

"Go to it, Yegg," Ballinger said. "You're in the clear."

One small snag presented itself. An almost solid wall of excited spectators stood behind the Yegg. However none of the crowd objected to somebody pushing past them if doing so allowed them to get closer to the rail and improved their view of the fight. Although a small man, the Yegg packed a fair amount of strength and used it to wriggle through the crowd. On reaching the rear, he paused for a moment to reconnoitre. He saw nothing to disturb him and so walked along the passage and halted at the door of Reckharts' office.

Ballinger did not follow the Yegg. While making their plans, the safe-breaker insisted on working alone and

Ballinger agreed that a watch must be kept so warning might reach the Yegg when the fight ended. There would be little or no danger as long as the women fought; but after it ended, the bouncer might remember his duty.

As the Yegg expected, he found the door locked. He had to pick open the lock while in full view of the crowd. The annoying aspect of the affair was that the Yegg had only himself to blame. Knowing that the contents of the safe could put him in trouble, Reckharts took precautions against theft. Being a wise man, he called in expert advice – and what more expert than a man who specialized in breaking into buildings. Using his knowledge in reverse as it were, the Yegg suggested means of protecting Reckharts' property, and now found himself cursing his own efficiency.

Knowing how little chance a thief would have of forcing an entry from inside the saloon – Reckharts now lived in a Streeterville mansion but his employees slept at the Blue Boar – the Yegg gave most of his attention to preventing access by means of the window of the office. Not that the door offered a flimsy barrier. Made of stout oak, it would withstand a battering ram and instead of an ordinary lever lock had the more efficient pin-tumbler variety designed by Linus Yale junior. The pin-tumbler mechanism contained six small cylinders which slid down into the keyhole, each cut at a different level and before the lock could be opened each of the cuts had to be perfectly aligned. The key for such a lock was made with a series of notched edges which, on being placed in position, pushed the pins into line and allowed the lock to be opened.

The Yegg did not possess a key with the necessary notches; but long experimentation had taught him how to get around such a deficiency. Taking a leather wallet from his pocket, he opened it and exposed a set of intricate and delicate tools used for picking locks. Selecting a tension tool, which looked like a tiny golf club, he placed the knobbed end into the lock and turned it so that pressure would be kept on the mechanism. Once he aligned the tumblers, the lock would snap open.

To pick a pin-tumbler lock took time and without a distraction the Yegg could never have accomplished it undetected.

Down below, Maggie and Sadie went on with their fight. Tight as two lovers, they churned over and over on the saw-dust-sprinkled floor. Fists flew; skirts rode up to expose shapely, thrashing legs in a manner which took the breath of almost every watching man, blouses parted company with waistbands and slid up over bare torsos.

In such a close-range tangle Sadie found herself getting the worst of the exchange. When underneath she took punishment in addition to having the blonde's weight crushing her and was forced to expend valuable energy in rolling Maggie from the upper position. All the while they rolled, fingers raked, clutched at and twisted flesh, or rained slaps and punches when not tearing at hair. Time after time Sadie turned Maggie from the top, gained the upper side, only to be rolled on to the floor and faced with the problem of doing it all over again.

A surging heave pitched Sadie over and Maggie threw a leg astride her, lurching up into the sitting position. First she tried to get at Sadie's face, but snapping teeth closed on her fingers once and she kept them clear when jerking them free. A quick grab saw Maggie gripping Sadie's hair. Twice the blonde raised Sadie's head and crashed it against the floor. Sadie thrashed and heaved in a desperate attempt to free herself. Raising her hands, she raked her nails down Maggie's shoulders and cloth ripped as she tore the blonde's blouse. Again Maggie brought Sadie's head down and sickening dizziness welled through the black-haired girl. Sadie's hands closed on flesh, fingers digging into Maggie's bust with

all her strength. Agony roared through the blonde and
her screams almost drowned the excited comments of
the crowd. Throwing herself to one side, Maggie tore
out of Sadie's grasp and landed on her side. Sadie flung
forward, wriggling until she sat behind Maggie. Placing
a foot on each of Maggie's shoulders, Sadie dug her
fingers into the blonde hair and began to pull with both
hands while shoving down with her feet.

Students of Sadie's form watched with eager an-
ticipation. Maggie shrieked and tried to sit up, reaching
for the hands in her hair, or the feet. Nothing Maggie
could do relieved her position and her feet beat on the
floor in a frenzy of agony.

Exerting all his will-power, Ballinger tore his eyes
from the fight and looked behind him to where the Yegg
crouched at Reckharts' office door and worked on the
lock.

A trickle of perspiration dribbled down the Yegg's
face, but he ignored its sting as he aligned the fifth pin
and carefully eased his pick into position to manipulate
the last. Working on a lock always put the Yegg through
a hard nervous strain and this time felt even worse. On
previous occasions only his liberty had been at stake.
Apprehension on the chore he handled in the Blue Boar
meant certain and painful death. The feeling existed,
but the Yegg refused to allow it to fluster him.

On the barroom floor, Maggie's screams rose to a
crescendo as she thrashed her body about in a wild attempt to free herself from the pressing feet and gripping
hands. Her attempts only made things worse and increased the pain. Then it happened. An extra hard pull
of Sadie's arms, and thrust of her legs, aided by a convulsive jerk by Maggie, tore a sizable hank of blonde
hair out by its roots. Maggie screeched like a soul in tor-
ment. The sudden releasing of her hair sent her body
sliding away from Sadie and her hands went up to clutch
at the bleeding top of her head. Pain drove through

Maggie and a look of almost maniacal rage twisted her face as she lurched to her feet, swinging around to look for Sadie.

Such had been the effort Sadie put into her pet trick – second only to her "goat butt" as a method of dealing with another woman – that she shot backwards as the hair came away in her hands. Wasting no time, Sadie thrust herself upright. She glanced down at the bloody-rooted hair still gripped in her hands. Then, seeing Maggie rise, she tossed her trophy on to the bar and prepared to defend herself.

Blood from Maggie's lacerated scalp ran down her face and into her left eye, half blinding her, but she attacked with hands flailing. Once again Sadie found herself having to use her fists and for a time had the best of the exchange. Then a savage smash to the face opened a gash over Sadie's right eye and blood ran down to nullify the advantage she gained from Maggie's head injury.

Staggering, gasping, reeling, the women closed with each other and locked in a savage, primeval wrestling session which took them to the floor once more. Ballinger saw Maggie rip off Sadie's blouse, leaving them both naked to the waist, and tore his eyes away to glance back along the passage.

With a final twist of his pick, the Yegg eased the last pin into position and the lock clicked open. Throwing a cautious look towards the balcony, and finding that nobody had eyes for anything but the raging fight below, the Yegg opened the door and stepped into Reckharts' office. He closed the door and bolted it so that if the bouncer recalled his duty and returned, a test would give the impression that the door remained locked. Turning, the Yegg walked across the room towards the Chatwood safe. Ignoring the comfortable, almost luxurious furnishings of the room, he went straight to work.

There were several ways in which a safe could be

opened without the use of a key, and the Yegg knew them all. In the early 1870's, metal development had not yet reached the stage when the "solid" safe – with top, bottom, two sides and the flanges at the rear bent out of a single sheet of steel – could be produced. So a favored method of opening was to drive wedges between the safe's body and door, making a gap into which the end of a crowbar could be inserted. Should the safe have one of the devices to prevent such a method, holes bored by the recently developed twist-drill could be filled with nitro-glycerine. This would, if used correctly and in the right quantity, blow open the door. If the safe-breaker did not care for those methods, he might bludgeon the lock's dial from the door with a small sledgehammer, and punch out the combination. If silence had to be maintained he could manipulate the combination dial with sensitive fingers until the clicking of the tumblers told him that he had found the right sequence.

A master at his trade, the Yegg could use any of the known methods – although he never cared to work with nitro. However, with one exception, each method required specialized equipment of a kind that a man could not easily conceal upon his person. Wedges, a sledge-hammer, crowbar, hacksaw, twist-drill could hardly be brought into the Blue Boar without attracting attention and exciting unwanted comment. Even without that, their use involved making too much noise. Manipulating the combination required no tools and was silent, but took far more time than the Yegg could devote to the task under the prevailing conditions.

Not that he needed to use any of the methods. On three occasions when the Yegg had been present, Reckharts had opened the safe for some reason. Being before Reckharts had met the Yegg's sister, and with his reputation for being straight, the Big Man took no precautions to prevent the safe-breaker from seeing the opening. Three times was more than enough for the Yegg to learn the combination. He did so automatically and with no thought of ever using his knowledge.

Capable fingers twirled the dial and its combination of numbers clicked the tumblers into place until the lock opened. Drawing open the door, the Yegg looked into the safe and gave a low hiss of satisfaction as he saw the contents. Swiftly he extracted four locked books and slipped them into special pockets built into his suit. Next he helped himself to a couple of bundles of documents and a thick sheaf of letters, hiding them about his person. Lastly he took three bundles of money and added them to the rest of his loot. Even should Reckharts go under, Chicago would be a mighty unhealthy location for the Yegg and all his family. Already his parents had left town and he aimed to follow them to their new home. After seeing his sister's fate, the Yegg decided to go straight and needed the money to help make a fresh start far from his old haunts.

After closing and locking the looted safe, he crossed the room and drew back the door's bolts. Cautiously he peered out through the crack. He saw nothing to disturb him, clearly the bouncer was too engrossed in watching the fight to attend to his duty. From the noise which welled up still, the Yegg knew that Maggie and Sadie were still battling. Thinking of how long it had taken him to open the door's lock and empty the safe, the Yegg guessed that neither woman would last much longer. If it came to a point, he felt surprised that even a pair of hardened termagants like Maggie and Sadie had fought for so long.

Hair matted and tangled with sweat, blood and sawdust; face and torso filthy, perspiration-soaked, scratched, bruised and bloody; naked to the waist and with her skirt torn to the hip at one side, Maggie reeled on her feet and landed a slap to an equally dishevelled and exhausted Sadie. Sadie staggered, croaking in pain and almost fell but managed at the last moment to keep her feet. As Maggie came stumbling forward, Sadie lowered her head and delivered a savage butt. The impact threw Maggie backwards and she would have crashed to the floor had she not hit the bar. She threw her arms on to the top of the counter, supporting the weight which threatened to buckle her legs and drop her unconscious to the floor. It seemed that Maggie was through at last. She hung on the bar, mouth trailing open and keening in agony.

For a long moment Sadie stood with feet braced apart, breasts heaving in the effort of sucking air into tortured lungs. Then she braced herself, lowered her head and prepared to deliver a *coup de grâce* with another of her 'goat butts'. Silence dropped on the room. All around the bouncers took firmer grips on their various persuaders, ready to halt any attempts by Maggie's supporters at helping their woman. Forward went Sadie with a rush, aiming her head to strike Maggie's bust. To the silent, watching crowd the end seemed inevitable. Maggie could never withstand such treatment in her present battered condition.

At the last moment Maggie twisted her body aside. Even if Sadie's pain-slowed brain saw the danger, it reacted far too poorly to save her. Unable to stop, she went head first into the bar. She hit the stout mahogany front with a shattering crash, bounced back and went crashing to the floor where she lay sprawled out, only the reaction of tortured muscles moving her legs and arms in jerking motions.

Barely conscious herself, Maggie stood staring down at Sadie for almost thirty seconds. Not a sound came from the watching crowd as Maggie gathered herself. Then a concerted gasp of apprehension and expectancy rose as the blonde sank to her knees at Sadie's side. A slap turned Sadie's face to one side and Maggie bent forward, her mouth opening and reaching down. Gripping the other woman's ear between her teeth, Maggie began to rise, took hold of Sadie by the arms and dragged her from the floor. Still gripping the ear, Maggie started to drag Sadie towards the batwing doors.

Pain drove through the waves of dizziness which filled Sadie and she started to struggle weakly. The grip on her ear tightened, grew more intense and she screamed. Desperately she threw her body from side to side in the gripping hands, trying to free herself from that agonizing hold. Her fingers raked at Maggie's thighs, leaving bloody furrows in the flesh, but Maggie refused to open her mouth. However the blonde removed her hands, letting Sadie's weight hang on the teeth-gripped ear. With the savagery that gave her her reputation Maggie clamped her teeth tighter on the trapped ear.

Suddenly Sadie fell free, screaming in agony and with blood pouring down the side of her face. Maggie staggered back a couple of paces, and as the other girl tried to rise, lunged in once more. Raising her left leg she delivered a stamping kick. With a flat 'splat!' which rang loud in the silent room, Maggie's bare foot smashed into Sadie's side and sent her reeling across the room towards the doors. Out of all control, Sadie smashed into the wall alongside the batwing doors, hung there for a moment and then slid to the floor.

Maggie stood with feet braced apart, swaying from side to side and staring through her one open eye towards the defeated Sadie. Opening her mouth, she spat something into her hand, turned and staggered to the bar. Amid cheers from her supporters, Maggie dropped a bloody human ear alongside the pickle jar. She had taken her trophy and won the fight.

CHAPTER FOUR

Reckharts' Loss, Chicago's Gain

Amidst cheers, Maggie turned from the bar and stared dazedly around the room. Her four gang associates came rushing up with beaming, delighted faces but she ignored them. Instead, she started to walk towards Reckharts' table to claim the prize for which she had fought, suffered and won. Realizing what Maggie had in mind, Reckharts looked sour and sick. No matter how the fight stimulated his lust, Maggie's appearance at that moment chilled any desires he might have felt towards her. Yet he knew that he must make the gesture when she reached him and the thought of what that would mean made him feel sick.

Maggie did not reach her prize. Before she took three steps in Reckharts' direction, her legs buckled under her and she crashed unconscious to the floor. Reckharts heaved a sigh of relief, thrust back his chair, rose and made the announcement expected of him.

"Belly up to the bar!" he called. "Drinks on the house!"

While willing to stand and give their acclaim to the winner, such an offer could not be overlooked. The spectators headed for the bar, swarming from all sides of the room and down from the balcony to make the most of the Big Man's largesse. The Pine Road Roller representatives and a doctor stayed at Maggie's side, while across the room a second medical man wound bandages around the bloody head of the loser.

Standing at the head of the stairs, Ballinger felt sickened at what he had brought about; although he knew that neither woman deserved any sympathy. Both had treated other women to brutal beatings without the law being able to touch them. In future they might tone down their efforts, knowing how it felt to be on the receiving end of the punishment. Then he remembered the Yegg and turned around. To his relief, he saw the safe-breaker approaching from the rear of the departing crowd. The bouncer had not returned to his post, but joined the other members of the saloon's pacifying squad to be ready to quell any disturbances arising from the fight.

A hand touched Ballinger's arm as he swung back to look down into the barroom. On turning, he found the Yegg had advanced to his side.

"Get anything, Yegg?" he asked.

"Everything you'll need," answered the Yegg. "And something for me."

"Then let's get the hell out of here," Ballinger suggested.

"I'd say that'd be the thing to do," agreed the safe-breaker.

Nobody in the barroom took the slightest notice of the two men as they descended to the ground floor. With the end of the fight, the bouncers allowed the spectators from the sidewalk to enter the room. Everybody was too busily engaged in trying to catch the bartenders attention and get a free drink to worry about two men leaving the room.

A short walk along the street brought Ballinger and the Yegg to a cab rank. Reckharts' place drew a sizable carriage trade and was situated in a better part of the Badlands, so cabs operated near to it. Taking a cab, Ballinger told the driver to make for the railroad depot. While the cab clattered through the streets, Ballinger accepted the loot. The Yegg picked open each book's lock and Ballinger studied their contents with interest. From what he saw, the detective figured that he held enough evidence to write *finis* to Reckharts.

"How about you, Yegg?" he asked. "What do you aim to do?"

"Get out of town as fast as I can go."

"Where're you going?"

"No offence, Ed," smiled the safe-breaker, "and not that I don't trust you, but I'm keeping that to myself."

"None took, Yegg," answered Ballinger. "If you ever need help, don't hesitate to call on me."

"Thanks."

The rest of the ride went by in silence and at the railroad depot Ballinger shook the Yegg's hand. Dropping from the cab, the Yegg mingled with the crowd and disappeared from Chicago forever. Ballinger also left the cab, let it drive away, and not until it had gone from sight did he try to find other transportation to the Police Headquarters. All the cab drivers operating from close to the Blue Boar held their posts at Reckharts' pleasure and the less one knew about the Yegg's movements, or Ballinger's, the better the detective would like it.

On arrival at headquarters, Ballinger went straight to Captain Mulrooney's office. There he presented his chief with the books, gave a quick résumé of the happenings at the Blue Boar and left Mulrooney studying the results of his work while he went to wash, shave and change his clothing.

"Reckon it was worth the risk, Cis?" Ballinger asked on his return, looking his usual self, an hour later.

"I've only just started going into these books," Mulrooney replied, "but I'd say they're more than worth it."

Knowing Reckharts' capabilities in evading the law, or finding loopholes in its structure, Mulrooney did not intend to rush into anything. While there was need for haste, he must also plan wisely and well if he wanted to make sure of the Big Man's capture. So Mulrooney settled down to make a careful study of the books and the more he read, the grimmer his face grew. In his big hands, Mulrooney held the most damning evidence against not only Reckharts and a number of criminals but a variety of apparently honest citizens and municipal officials.

"This's big, Ed," he breathed. "Too big for us to go alone on. I'm going to bring in the Chief and the mayor."

"We can't risk waiting too long," Ballinger answered.

"I dropped a hint to them to stick around the building and they took it, so getting them won't be any bother."

"Uh-huh. Say, I didn't see any sign of Abe Cohen's name in the books."

"Cohen isn't one of Reckharts' men," Mulrooney pointed out.

"Looks that way," agreed Ballinger. "I'd sure have liked to nail him along with the rest."

Although Abe Cohen, an organizer of child criminals and fence for stolen property, slipped the net this time, Ballinger did eventually bring him to justice.*

."Don't be a hog, Ed," grinned Mulrooney, walking towards his office door. "If we only haul in everybody named in the books, we'll have a full house in the cells."

At that time Chicago's top municipal officials, the mayor and chief of police, had each sworn to clean up their city. A pair of tough Irishmen, Mayor O'Bryan and Chief Gill, respected Mulrooney and backed him in every way possible. Without asking any questions, they joined the two detectives in Mulrooney's office and went through the books carefully.

"How about that bundle of letters?" Gill asked, waving a hand towards part of the Yegg's loot.

"I'll see they get back to their owners," Mulrooney

* Told in *The Fortune Hunters* by J. T. Edson.

answered. "A lot of folk'll sleep easier for seeing them."

Gill and O'Bryan went through the books and at last the chief of police nodded grimly. "Go to it, Cis. This's what we've been waiting for. Take every man you want and bring them all in."

"Ed," Mulrooney said. "Fetch Joe Stafford, Dan McCall, Sergeants Schmidt, Lockyer, Guintaio and Vogue."

"How about Goldstein and Carrela?" asked Ballinger, mentioning two further members of the Detective Bureau.

"They won't be going with us," replied the captain, nodding to the books. "Reckharts meant to take everybody, and I mean everybody, with him if he fell."

"So Goldstein and Carrela are in it," growled Ballinger.

"Up to their necks."

"What'll we do about them?"

"We've got a nice little room upstairs, Ed," O'Bryan put in. "It's just waiting to be filled. And we'll have to fill it to stop any word reaching Reckharts that we're on to him."

Turning, Ballinger left the room. He moved fast, gathering in the men Mulrooney named and bringing them to the captain's office. Quickly Mulrooney explained to the men what had happened. Admiring glances and grins went to Ballinger, but Mulrooney wasted no time while congratulations passed among his subordinates. Eagerness showed on every face, for the detectives brought in each wanted to see the organized crime broken in Chicago. Swiftly Mulrooney assigned each man a duty. A number of arrests must be made in the building and done speedily, so that none of Reckharts' employees on the municipal payroll managed to escape and give him warning.

"Go to it, boys," Mulrooney finally ordered. "Come on, Ed. We'll clean our house."

"You'd best go ready for trouble," O'Bryan warned.

"Reckon we had at that," grinned Mulrooney and opened his desk drawer to take out a plaited leather, lead-loaded billy which assisted him in many a rough arrest.

Before going to interview Goldstein and Carrela Ballinger went into the small office he shared with another lieutenant. Opening the drawer of his desk, he took out a twenty-inch long baton that had accompanied him into more than one tight spot and in the use of which he could claim to be something of a master. Made of stout hickory, the club showed a few dents and scars on its length and formed a mighty deadly weapon in his skilled hands. Placing the baton's leather thong over his right thumb so it hung crossed over the back of his hand, Ballinger turned his palm inwards and grasped the shaped handle so that the thumb pointed parallel to the stick. Being correctly adjusted to Ballinger's size, the thong ensured that he gripped the handle firmly and in a manner which allowed him to wield it in freedom.

A Smith and Wesson Army No. I revolver shared the drawer with the baton. Only as an afterthought did Ballinger take out the small .32 calibre revolver and drop it into his pocket. Despite the fact that Chicago drew a considerable portion of its wealth from the western cattle industry, it was fast throwing off the mantle of the frontier city and had grown far beyond its wild, wide-open pioneer days. For the most part its criminals went about their work armed with razors, knives, brass knuckles, pick handles or clubs. Due to the size of most handguns at that time, concealment posed too great a problem for a criminal and only rarely did one go about his business carrying a firearm. Nor were the occasional gun-toters skilled in the use of their weapons. True the odd western man did make an appearance, but so infrequently as to be an almost negligible factor.

Working with one eye on the taxpayers' money, the Police Department did not go to the expense of issuing its men with revolvers, although an armory of weapons was available in case of emergency. While the department permitted any of its officers to purchase their own guns, it neither paid for ammunition nor offered any inducement for the man to become skilled in the weapon's use. So, although he spent enough of his pay on bullets to become proficient – by city standards – with the Smith and Wesson, Ballinger lay his emphasis on the baton and merely pocketed the revolver in the unlikely event that he might need it.

With the collection of his arms attended to, Ballinger joined Mulrooney and together they went to a room at the other end of the passage. After knocking, Mulrooney pushed open the door and entered with Ballinger on his heels.

Lieutenant Reuben Goldstein and Sergeant Stephen Carrela were in the office, a small room no better furnished or equipped than that in which Ballinger worked. Although they had heard some coming and going in the passage, neither man had troubled to look out of their door and learn what had happened. Both glanced first at Mulrooney, then towards Ballinger as he followed the captain towards the desk.

"Hi, Captain!" Goldstein greeted sullenly, knowing that neither of his visitors particularly cared for him or his methods.

"How're things, Lieutenant?" asked Mulrooney. "Or should I say 'Mr. Steiner'?"

Anger and a hint of fear showed on Goldstein's face. Being a smarter man than the detective Ballinger caught out, Goldstein never gave any hint that he augmented his salary by serving the Big Man. Any money due to him passed directly into a bank account taken out under the name of Steiner – a fact which he fondly believed to be a secret shared only by Reckharts.

"I don't know what you mean," he mumbled.

"How about you, Carrela?" Mulrooney inquired, turning his eyes to the tall, surly-looking sergeant. "Or do I call you 'Boldini'?"

"What did Sammy Hook call you the night you killed him resisting arrest, Carrela?" growled Ballinger. "Just like Reckharts told you to do."

Giving a snarl, Goldstein jerked open the desk drawer and shot his hand inside to the butt of a revolver. Ballinger knew of the other man's weapon and moved fast to prevent its appearance. Up and out shot Ballinger's right arm, using the baton with that snapping flick of the wrist motion which proved far more effective than a wild swing. Knowing the danger of striking at the head, Ballinger brought his baton down hard against Goldstein's collar bone. Such a blow was more effective, and less liable to produce a serious or fatal injury than one landing on the skull. While he hated a dishonest policeman, Ballinger did not want the other's death on his conscience.

While still in the act of rising and drawing his gun, Goldstein took the impact of the baton on his shoulder. Pain knifed through him, his right arm and hand went numb and he could not raise the revolver or even grasp its butt. Flopping back into his chair, Goldstein sat rigid and dazed.

Letting out a snarl, Carrela lunged from where he had been standing by the wall. He flung himself at Mulrooney and learned what many another man knew; while big, bulky and showing considerable grey in his short-cropped hair, Captain Mulrooney could move with a speed that one much younger might envy. Move fast and hit with the power of a mule-kick. Side-stepping Carrela's rush, Mulrooney threw his right at the other's head. Hard knuckles, powered by a muscular body, crashed into the side of Carrela's jaw. Taken by surprise and not expecting his attack to miss, Carrela shot across the room to crash into his dazed superior. Unable to stand the weight of two such hefty men, Goldstein's chair collapsed under him and precipitated them both to the floor.

Before either of the dazed men could recover or drive thoughts into their spinning heads, Ballinger took out his handcuffs and moved forward. Long training and practice had taught him how to deal with such a situation. Bending down, he caught Goldstein's left wrist and clamped home the jaws of one cuff. Then he took Carrela's arm and secured it to Goldstein. Stepping back, Ballinger surveyed his work with a satisfied expression.

"That's fixed them," he said

"Let's hope that the others have done their part," Mulrooney answered. "On your feet, me beauties, we've a nice little room upstairs for you."

Bending down, the burly captain laid hold of Goldstein and Carrela's collars to haul them erect. Still dazed, neither made any resistance or objections to their treatment and were hustled towards the office door.

Already the first fruits of the other raids showed in men being escorted in the direction of the upper floor cells. Mulrooney watched the prisoners go by and felt cold anger as he realized why so many attempts to capture Reckharts' top men failed. Almost every move made by the law had been known to one or more of the Big Man's hired help. Two of the four regular desk sergeants drew pay from Reckharts and they had access to the blotter, the official log of arrests and arrested persons, from which so much information could be drawn. Now the two marched handcuffed together, their faces showing bewildered dismay at being caught out.

Not all the arrested men belonged to the Police Department. Reckharts' loss had been Chicago's gain with a vengeance and a number of municipal officials who served in capacities the Big Man found useful now marched up the stairs towards the cell block on the top floor. One way and another, Chicago would be a cleaner, better town as a result of the Yegg and Ballinger's work that day.

"That's all of 'em who're on watch and in the building, sir," Lieutenant Stafford announced, as he came to Mulrooney's side and held out a sheet of paper on which was listed a number of names. "The rest are off watch and at their homes. Do I get men out to pick them up?"

"Not yet. We've stopped any chance of word getting out to Reckharts. Now we'd best get after the Big Man. Hey, where's Werner?"

"Coming now," answered Stafford flatly and nodded to where two patrolmen supported and half-dragged, half-carried a uniformed lieutenant up the stairs.

"What happened to him?" growled Mulrooney.

"The darlin' met wid an accident, sir," replied one of the patrolmen. "Sure and when we was a-walking him up here, he made a run for the door."

"Must've tripped over something, Cap'n darlin'," went on the second.

"He's quiet enough now," finished the first.

"Looks that way," Mulrooney said dryly. "Take him up and find him a nice quiet corner to lie in."

"We'll do that, so we will," promised the first patrolman and continued on his way upstairs.

"Let go of me!" screeched a tinny voice.

Struggling futilely in the grasp of a burly detective, a thin, weedy and well-dressed little man raised his objections as he came into view. Just as they passed where Ballinger and Mulrooney stood, the little man gave up his attempts to escape from the detective's grasp. Turning his gaze towards Mulrooney, and trying to assume an air of injured, outraged innocence, the man changed his tactics.

"Tell this officer to unhand me, Captain Mulrooney!" he yelled. "The fool says he's arresting me."

"Looks like he is, too," Mulrooney agreed.

"This is an outrage!" squalled the man. "I'll have somebody's badge for it, see if I don't. Wait until Mayor O'Bryan hears about this."

The man was a senior clerk on the mayor's staff and a well-paid employee of Reckharts.

"He's heard," replied Mulrooney cheerfully. "Mentioned your name when he was talking about that construction contract for the Clanton Street School."

Sick anxiety wiped the righteous indignation from the man's face as he remembered that his assistance enabled an entirely unworthy building company to gain the contract to build a new school in the city.

"I – I want to see my lawyer," he mumbled.

"We'll tend to it," Mulrooney promised. "What's his name?"

"The Honourable Anthony Reckharts," the man replied, sounding hopeful as he thought of other cases his lawyer successfully defended.

"Now don't that beat all," grinned Mulrooney. "We were just going to fetch him down here."

Chuckling at his superior's unsubtle joke, the detective tightened his grip on the prisoner's arm and hustled him upstairs.

Now that word could not reach Reckharts, Mulrooney reported to Mayor O'Bryan and Chief Gill. They expressed their entire satisfaction and Gill assumed command. Every available man, both uniformed and detective, stood by ready to enter the waiting four-horse paddy-wagons. A force of mounted policemen waited with their horses to provide a mobile strike force and to hold back such members of the public as might be attracted to the Blue Boar when the raid began.

Eager faces looked at Gill as he told the assembled men what they were going to do. Not all of the men had the interests of justice at heart, some of them revelled in the thought of action, the chance of a good fight, or merely in a change from the dull routine of walking a beat.

As Gill finished speaking, and before the men could enter the paddy-wagons, Mayor O'Bryan strolled out of the building. He had removed his jacket and rolled up his shirt sleeves to expose brawny arms. In his right hand swung a police baton, twirling on its supporting thong with the deft ease of a practicing patrolman's night stick.

"All right, me buckoes," he said. "You voted me in to clean up our city. So I'm coming with you to help to do it."

Amid cheers and encouraging yells, O'Bryan swung into the leading paddy-wagon followed by Gill, Mulrooney and Ballinger. Soon the cavalcade of law enforcement went streaming out of headquarters and headed across town towards the Blue Boar.

Sitting in the foremost paddy-wagon, Ballinger fumed at the amount of time which had elapsed since he left the Blue Boar. Yet the delay could not be avoided. He hoped it would not give Reckharts time to open the safe and discover the loss. If that happened, the Big Man might even now escape.

CHAPTER FIVE

The Big Man Shows Loyalty to his Followers

So far the law's luck had been exceptionally good and everything fell just as Ballinger hoped it would. Caught unawares by the swift action of Mulrooney's men, not one of the city hall grafters succeeded in sending a word of warning to Reckharts. Nor did Reckharts find any need to go up to his private office for some considerable time after the fight had ended.

Unfortunately, as every gambler knows, luck runs in circles. After favoring the forces of law and order, the gods of chance figured it was time that they turned the wheel and let Reckharts have his share.

The end of the fight signalled the start of a sizable celebration at the Blue Boar. Although both of the fighters had been carried off to receive medical care for their numerous injuries, the spectators showed no desire to disperse. Such an event as the battle just witnessed could not soon be cast aside and forgotten. It needed to be discussed, relived in words – any attempt to relive the fight in deeds was swiftly and effectively halted by Reckharts' bouncers.

At the bar, the Pine Road Rollers detachment toasted their success and received the acclaim of all and sundry. Separated by a bunch of customers and a pair of bulky, watchful bouncers, the East Stockyard boys, and their two remaining girls, drowned their sorrows.

47

All around the room men and women drank, laughed, talked; old enmities were forgotten in the heady excitement raised by watching the fight and kept flowing under the stimulus of the drinks they bought – Reckharts' largesse did not extend beyond the first round he called. While wanting his guests to enjoy themselves, he had no intention of allowing them to do so at his expense.

Lord and monarch of all he surveyed, Reckharts sat with the elite at his table. Long practice had taught him to take one drink while his companions sank three, four or more, yet still appear to be drinking level with them but retaining the full control of his faculties. In that way, he stayed sober and in a position to watch or listen to his guests, learning how they really felt when liquor loosened their tongues. At Reckharts' side, the tall, tanned man who so interested Ballinger sat quietly and drank neat whisky without showing any particular effect beyond having removed his collar and tie. The rest of the occupants of the Big Man's table showed nothing but a desire to enjoy themselves.

For almost three hours after the end of the fight, the law's good fortune continued to hold. Almost every top member of Reckharts' organization attended the fight and remained with their boss after its conclusion. As none of the various sub-leaders trusted the others when absent, they all meant to stick it out to the bitter end, which would present the forces of law and order with a good-sized haul.

It was the Honorable Judge Grossmeyer who ended the law's lucky streak. As befitted a person of his importance, Grossmeyer shared the Big Man's table and sat at Reckharts' left hand. All around the good judge gathered the cream of criminal Chicago, although it must be confessed that he did not particularly care for the idea of having his back slapped or ribs poked by such men. However he had to put up with such treatment as part-payment – and very good pay too – in his employment on Reckharts' staff.

Despite the joviality around him, Grossmeyer felt unhappy and disturbed. He had a problem of some importance on his mind, one which must receive speedy attention. Making up his mind, the judge turned to Reckharts.

"May I speak with you in private for a moment, Tony?" he asked.

"Any time, your honor," boomed Reckharts magnanimously. "What is it?"

"Er – well, I—"

"Oh!" grinned Reckharts, remembering other times when Grossmeyer acted in the same furtive manner. "I see."

Then he found that he did not see after all. Usually the judge's attitude heralded a request that some young lady be brought over, introduced and made amenable to his honor's wishes.

"Which one?" asked Reckharts, as he and the judge drew out of earshot of the big table.

"Which one—?" began the judge, sounding puzzled. Then the light broke in. "Oh! It's not that. I bet five hundred dollars that Sadie – er, Miss Barkis won—"

"And you want me to loan you the money to pay?" guessed Reckharts.

That had not been the judge's intention. Rather he hoped that Reckharts would bring pressure to bear and have the bet annulled. However he knew better than to argue. Grossmeyer realized that he gave the Big Man valuable aid, but also that his past assistance made him Reckhart's slave in all things. So he nodded his agreement, knowing that Reckharts would never demand the return of the money.

Reaching towards his inside pocket, Reckharts remembered that he had followed his usual practice of leaving his money in the safe upstairs. Caution made him avoid carrying money with him. Not that he need fear robbery; the dip had not been born in Chicago who dare pick the Big Man's pocket. The real reason for Reckharts' reluctance to carry money stemmed from his objection to make a requested loan and the knowledge that a refusal might offend the asker. However the judge was a special case, his official position giving him the means to smooth the Big Man's path in many ways. Refusing to settle Grossmeyer's debt of honor might lead to dissatisfaction and strife, something Reckharts always tried to avoid.

"I seem to have left my wallet upstairs, your honor," he purred. "Just sit down for a moment and I'll fetch it."

Seeing Reckharts turn from the table the tall, tanned man came to his feet. Without a word to the others, he walked after the departing Reckharts. Normally Mugs O'Toole would have been present and acted in just the same manner. The discrepancy aroused the interest of a well-dressed man who specialized in consorting with, and blackmailing, rich, elderly ladies.

"Where might Mugsy be?" he inquired.

"Dunno," grunted the burly hard-case at his side. "Ain't seen him all day."

"Who's that tall jasper with the Big Man?" pressed the blackmailer.

"He ain't said," was the informative reply. "Acts like he's took Mugsy's place though. But I can't see how."

"Talks like them rebs who used to guard us prisoners in the war," remarked an organizer of a successful Great Lakes pirate gang.

"Could be one of them Western outlaws we keep reading about," the hard-case guessed. "Maybe wants the Big Man to plan something for him."

"Sure looks like he's meaning to stick by the Big Man," grinned the pirate. "Can't see old Mugsy going along with that."

"I can't see Mugsy missing the fight," the black-mailer stated. "Wasn't that something to see though."

"Sure was. I can't see why old Mugsy missed it," answered the pirate.

"Maybe he couldn't help missing it," remarked the leader of a pickpocket mob.

"What's that mean?" asked the blackmailer, knowing the other had been in the Blue Boar since early morning.

"Nothing much," the pickpocket answered. "Only if I was you, I'd wouldn't sit holding my breath waiting for Mugsy to show."

Although the others would have liked to know the meaning behind the dip's cryptic remark, they chose to ignore the matter. At that moment a singer came on to the stage and the matter was dropped.

Not knowing or caring about the interest his new colleague aroused among his guests, Reckharts passed through the crowd and walked upstairs. The tall man followed with long strides and watchful attention to the people who approached their host to congratulate him on a fine piece of entertainment. On reaching the head of the stairs, Reckharts saw that his bouncer no longer stood guard on the passage. Not that he should be, his orders were to watch the room during the time most folks' attention stayed on the fight, then join the other bouncers ready to quell any trouble. Reckharts had been aware of the interest such a fight would have and saw the danger of having such a large crowd in the building when most of his staff would be engrossed and unlikely to keep a watchful eye on the place. So, although his ego insisted that nobody would dare to rob the Big Man, he took precautions.

Taking out his keys, he studied the door's lock but saw nothing changed in it. Picking open a lock, as the Yegg had done it, left the mechanism in working order and Reckharts suspected nothing as he inserted, then turned the key. Nothing in the office gave the slightest hint of a visitor and without a suspicion in the world Reckharts manipulated the safe's dial. He drew open the door.

"Trust Grossmeyer to lose money and expect somebody else to p—" he began.

The words chopped off as he saw the denuded state of the safe's interior. For a few moments he fought to discredit the evidence of his eyes. Then the full gravity of the situation struck home and drove pangs of fear through him. Some three thousand dollars had been in the safe when he last locked it but that loss did not worry him unduly. The money was only a drop in the ocean, a reserve kept handy for a variety of purposes. The money could be replaced easily. What filled Reckharts with such concern was the loss of a sheaf of blackmail letters and those damning books in which he kept much, in fact most, of his business transactions recorded. While the books had been his insurance against betrayal, and an effective means of keeping his underlings in line, Reckharts fully realized just how they would touch him should they fall into the wrong hands.

"What's up?" asked the tall man.

"I – ins – ins – in – " Reckharts answered, sounding like a turkey gobbling and unable to produce anything more coherent.

Stepping forward, the man shoved by Reckharts and looked into the safe.

"I'd say that somebody's been and emptied it," he drawled laconically.

Then a realization of just what that entailed struck the man. Turning, he crossed the room and opened the door, bending to examine the lock. After a close scrutiny of the lock, he straightened up and walked back to the safe once more. All through the man's movements, Reckharts remained where he had been, staring as if mesmerized at the empty safe. While he ran a criminal empire second to none, Reckharts' brains, organizing ability and knowledge of how to find loopholes in the fabric of the law, rather than toughness and cold courage, gave him his place in life. The sight of the looted safe – along with the knowledge of what it meant – unnerved him and rendered him incapable of thought or action.

Not so the tall man. He gave the room a long, careful study, crossing to open the closet and search its interior, then examining the window with the same thoroughness he showed in checking the door's lock. At last he walked back to the safe, laid hold of Reckharts' arm and shook him hard.

"Come out of it, man!" he snapped, his voice cold and hard. "Start thinking, or it's your neck, Reckharts."

No man of Reckharts' acquaintance would have dared to perform such an impious act as laying hands upon him. However the tall, tanned stranger did so and his lack of respect helped get through the fear which held Reckharts immobile. That and the cold truth in the words. If Reckharts did not think, and think fast, his liberty and maybe his life would be forfeit.

"Who could have done it?" Reckharts groaned.

"You know this range better'n I do," the man replied. "Way I see it, the *hombre* who opened that door knew what he was doing and wasn't year-old stock at the game. That door was locked when we come in here."

"And the lock wasn't broken," Reckharts agreed. "But he told me that a pin-tumbler lock couldn't—"

Then he stopped speaking as he remembered who gave him advice about the security of his property.

"Who told you?" asked the man.

"You haven't met him and don't know him, Mr. Lash. I had a man tell me how to make the office safe from robbery. But he wouldn't—"

"Somebody has," Jason Lash pointed out. "You ever give this feller who told you any cause to do it himself?"

Although not willing to admit the fact, Reckharts knew he had given the Yegg very excellent cause to hate him and want revenge. Yet there did not appear to be any way in which the Yegg could have heard of his sister's death. There had been no mention of the body's discovery either verbally or in the newspapers, and Reckharts had given strict instructions for its disposal – the task had failed that. Word reached Reckharts that the Yegg did not bring off the robbery and fall into the trap, but the Big Man had thought little about it until seeing the empty safe and being questioned by Lash. Suppose that the Yegg—

Reckharts shook his head, trying to hide the thoughts or drive them away. It seemed unlikely that the Yegg would take such a terrific risk, knowing the defenses of the office. Yet had it been such a risk? Probably even the bouncer assigned to guarding the passage left his post to watch the fight. With such an attraction down below, nobody would have eyes for anything else.

"Was this feller in today?" asked Lash, even as the question entered Reckharts' head.

"I can't remember seeing him. He never came to the table, that I'm sure of. And he always has before."

Apparently Lash accepted that Reckharts did give the man in question reason to hate him and so dropped the matter, for which Reckharts felt grateful.

"Reckon we'd best ask somebody who'll *know* for sure," drawled Lash. "I'll get that Lighthouse *hombre* up here."

"Do that," Reckharts agreed.

Crossing to the door, Lash left the room and at the end of the passage told one of the girls to take word downstairs that Lighthouse was wanted in the office. On his return, Lash resumed the subject of the safe's illegal opening.

"Could this Yegg jasper have opened it?"

"He's opened harder than this."

"Just what was in the safe?"

"Enough to jail or hang every man at that table downstairs, and more."

"Any money?"

"Some. But it's the other missing stuff that worries me."

"Would this feller take it to the law?" asked Lash.

"He's never been anything but straight," Reckharts answered. "I can't—"

"Close up that door, there's somebody coming!"

Ignoring the propriety of any man giving him orders in his own office, Reckharts closed the safe door. He glanced towards the office's door and saw the familiar shape of Lighthouse approaching. By the time the bartender entered, Reckharts had regained his self-control.

"You wanted me, boss?" asked Lighthouse.

"Sure. Did the Yegg come in today?"

"Yep. Come just afore the fight started."

"Was he alone?" Lash put in.

"No. Got another feller with him," answered Lighthouse, after glancing at Reckharts. "Is something up, boss?"

"Should there be?" Reckharts growled. "Who was the feller with the Yegg?"

"Looked like the engineer off a boat," Lighthouse replied.

"Why didn't he come over to the table?" asked Reckharts.

"Don't reckon he thought the feller he was with'd fit in. You want the Yegg for something, boss?"

"Is he still here?" Reckharts breathed.

"Can't say as I've seen him," Lighthouse admitted. "Him and the other feller came up on the balcony. Were stood right at the head of the stairs."

"All the time?" drawled Lash.

"I don't know. I wasn't watching 'em. Could go down and look for them, boss."

"Do that," confirmed Reckharts. "If they're here, ask them to come up – and make sure they come."

Giving a nod, and refraining from asking any more questions, Lighthouse turned and walked from the office. In a few moments he returned.

"Can't see any sign of 'em, boss," he reported.

"You-all know this feller with the Yegg?" asked Lash.

"Thought he looked a mite familiar," Lighthouse admitted. "Only I couldn't place him. Maybe he's been in before."

"That's likely," agreed Lash, and threw a warning glance at Reckharts before the other could ask any of the questions boiling inside him. "If either the Yegg or his pard come in, let us know."

"Sure," grunted Lighthouse, and, seeing that the others did not want him any more, turned to leave the room.

"I should've asked him if he thought the feller with the Yegg was an elbow," Reckharts said, after the door closed on Lighthouse.

"Does the Yegg usually ride herd with John Law?" inquired Lash mildly.

"No. He's always been straight."

"Then you ask Lighthouse a question like that and you're going to start him thinking even more than he's doing now. We don't want to spook that bunch downstairs. There might be nothing in the robbery, except that he went for money. The fight ended a fair piece back and no posse's shown yet."

"It'd take them time to go through the books, get organized and come," Reckharts pointed out.

"Likely. Which means that you've a chance to make plans afore they get here. I reckon you don't aim to stand and make a fight of it?"

"Of course not!"

"Then we have to get clear without any fuss. Did he empty the safe?"

"Near enough. That short—"

"Cussing him when he's not here won't help," Lash

said. "And it wastes time. If he's given the books to the law, you're going to have to run and run a fair ways. Why not run down into my country and look into the deal I offered?"

Suspicion flooded into Reckharts' head. On his arrival, Lash had made certain proposals which Reckharts had not considered worthwhile, although the tall man seemed eager to have them put into being. How eager, Mugs O'Toole might have been able to say. Maybe Lash —no. That would be impossible for a number of reasons. And even if the suspicion should have a solid foundation, Reckharts did not intend to air his views after a certain demonstration he had witnessed of one of Lash's specialized skills.

"All right," Reckharts answered. "I'll do that. But only if the law has the books."

"Let's get out of here, just in case," suggested Lash. "How're you set for money?"

"The books don't tell where I've banked any. The details of my bank accounts are in the safe at my home."

"Unless that Yegg *hombre* went there too."

A look of horror came to Reckharts' face as a thought struck him. "The Yegg fitted out the house for me too!"

"Then the sooner we get there, the better," Lash stated.

"We can get a cab along the street," Reckharts answered.

"Let's go then."

"I need five hundred to pay off a gambling debt for Grossmeyer. That's what I came up for and he might see us leaving."

"I'll tend to him if he does," drawled Lash, then grinned at the startled and frightened expression which came to Reckharts' face. "With money, what else?"

Taking a well-filled wallet from his jacket, Lash peeled off five hundred dollars and passed them to Reckharts. Then they left the office and went on to the balcony. A singer on the stage held the attention of most of the crowd, including Grossmeyer, so the two men went downstairs and made for the door instead of returning to their table.

"Mr. Reckharts," said the leader of the Pine Road Rollers contingent, turning from the bar. "Maggie's been fixed up by the doc, and gone home. She wants for you to go see her."

"Not right now," Reckharts answered, then realized that he spoke too quickly and tried to smooth over any ill-feeling. "I – I'm just going down town to buy her a present for her victory."

"I'll tell her then," grinned the man and returned to the bar.

Although the street outside the Blue Boar was still busy, the crowd which gathered to witness the fight had dispersed. The only sign of law and order appeared to be a beat-walking patrolman who drew small donations from Lighthouse in return for being blind to certain comings and goings and also lending an air of authority when trouble threatened in the saloon. For a moment Reckharts thought of stopping the man and asking questions, but saw the folly of such an action. If a humble, and not very bright, patrolman knew of danger, so would others higher up the law's social scale. Surely at least one of his contacts at headquarters would have slipped the net and brought word if the books had fallen into the hands of the law.

Hailing a passing cab, Reckharts and Lash climbed inside. The Big Man gave the driver instructions and they began to move away from the Blue Boar. After the cab started moving, Reckharts let out a deep sigh. However before they had gone a hundred yards, he glanced back and gave a low exclamation. Turning to look through the rear window, Lash saw three paddy-wagons swing into sight and come to a halt before the saloon, each disgorging uniformed and plain clothed officers.

"We only just made it!" breathed Reckharts.

"Yep," agreed Lash calmly. "But we'll have a fair head start before they know we've gone. Your house first, then out of town."

"They'll be watching the railroad depot and the docks," Reckharts warned.

"Likely. Still we're not going to either."

"Then how—?"

"We'll do it my way. Pick up a couple of good hosses at a livery barn I've found and go across country until we're clear. Then we'll think about the railroad."

As a city-dweller, the idea of making an escape on horseback and across the open country had never occurred to Reckharts. To him, flight always meant either by train or Great Lakes side-wheeler. However he saw the advantage in Lash's plan. Alone Reckharts knew he could not make such a trip, but felt certain that his companion possessed the necessary skill to bring them through.

"We'll do what you say," he told Lash. "And I'll go with you to try that idea of yours."

"You won't regret it," drawled Lash, "as long as you don't start putting down names in your tally book when you get there."

CHAPTER SIX

Lash's Trade

None of the crowd at the Blue Boar missed their departed host, being fully occupied with their own affairs. Even Judge Grossmeyer paid no attention to Reckharts' continued absence for the entertainer on the stage sang and dressed in an attractive manner.

Not even the thunder of hooves and rumbling of wheels outside distracted the saloon's occupants to any great extent. While the various people walking the street saw the approaching paddy-wagons, none thought to enter the Blue Boar and give a warning. Such visits by the law had never been such an unusual sight as to excite comment in the Badlands, although the raiding party appeared to be one of great strength. If there was speculation as to the raid's destination, nobody suspected it would be directed at the Big Man's saloon. So, apart from the hurried disappearance of a few people, none of the strollers and idlers on the street took more than a casual interest.

Halting in a line before the Blue Boar, each wagon disgorged its occupants. Swiftly the men formed up into four groups, while the mounted officers swung into position. Two of the groups ran around the building to the right, the first halting at the side entrance and the second making for the rear. While the third section went to cover the left of the building, Gill, Mulrooney and

Ballinger prepared to go in at the front with the remainder.

A whistle shrilled at the right, followed by another telling that the left flank was covered and a moment later the rear detachment signified their presence in the same manner.

"Let's go!" Gill ordered, raising his whistle to his lips and blowing a blast in reply.

The band's music died to an uncertain halt as its musicians saw the batwing doors burst open and policemen enter. Talk and noise ebbed away, every eye turning to where the law made its dramatic appearance. Rising from their seats, two men made hurried and separate rushes for the side entrances; only to find their way blocked.

"Just sit still, all of yez!" boomed Gill's bull voice. " 'Tis only some of you we want."

Following on the heels of merriment and celebration, the cold, grim, purposeful approach of the police chilled even the roughest of the crowd. The lesser lights looked to the Big Man's table for guidance; but Reckharts' guests turned their eyes towards the balcony and waited to see what their boss wanted them to do, or how he handled the situation. Not one of them doubted for a moment that Reckharts would come from his office and settle the matter to their satisfaction.

Possibly Grossmeyer first realized that all might not be well. As a member of the Bar, he reckoned to know his business and was aware that such a raid called for legal warrants. That such warrants could be sworn out without Reckharts receiving ample warning struck the judge as significant. Deciding that all might not be as secure as he liked, Grossmeyer eased back his chair and started to rise. By that time Gill, Mulrooney and Ballinger had almost reached the Big Man's table.

"Don't go, your honor," Gill said quietly, but his words, carried around the room. "You're one of the men we want."

"I – I don't know what you mean," Grossmeyer gulped.

"You're in good company here," the chief of police explained. "Among thieves."

A sudden chill came over Grossmeyer, for he knew that under normal circumstances no municipal employee, even one in such a high position, would dare address him in such a manner. Only with certain evidence would Gill make such a statement, yet he could hardly have any evidence – but if not, why had he come to the Blue Boar and with so many men at his back? A good proportion of both morning and afternoon watch officers appeared to be present.

Ignoring Grossmeyer after his comment, Gill looked around the table. Every man present would occupy a cell once arrested, but he wanted to take out the leaders capable of rousing the crowd and organizing full-scale resistance.

"All right, Vargas, Minter, Paxley," he said. "On your feet. You're under arrest."

"Sure," Vargas, the pirate, replied and started to rise with an amiable grin – his hand slipping under his reefer jacket.

Life a flash Mulrooney raised and swung his baton. He knew that the pirate carried a gun in the waistband and took no chances. Caught on top of the head by the baton, Vargas dropped without a sound. The hard-case known as Minter had begun to thrust aside his chair even as Vargas made his move, and met with no better success. Gill knew that Minter specialized in robbery that was always accompanied by violence and carried a razor in a handy place to enforce his will on others. A baton in the hand proved to be worth any number of hidden razors at that moment. Caught across the side of the head, Minter pitched sideways, crashed into the burly Paxley who tended to be a slow thinker and was just rising. Before Paxley could untangle himself, a patrolman bounced a baton off the top of his head and caused him to lose all interest in the affair.

The blackmailer's chair slid back and he began to rise. While watching the opening moves, Ballinger stood holding his baton in a tension grip. He kept his left hand holding the striking end of the baton, while the right forced it against the grip. On being released by the left, the club would shoot forward suddenly and with some power – as the blackmailer discovered. Without waiting to discover what the man's intentions might be, Ballinger flicked clear his left hand and the baton lashed out. Bringing it around and up, Ballinger smashed the stout timber full into the blackmailer's handsome face. From Reckharts' books and the letters recovered, Ballinger knew the man for what he was; it did not make him feel well disposed to him. The blackmailer used his good looks as a bait to attract elderly women and set them up for his vicious trade. Only he would never do so again. While a skilled dentist might have replaced the smashed teeth, medical science had not yet advanced to the stage where the baton-broken nose could be brought back to its original classic lines. Reeling back, his nose and mouth gushing blood, the blackmailer went down at the feet of an unsympathetic patrolman who bent and slapped home a pair of handcuffs.

So sudden had been the handling of the men that the crowd still remained motionless and made no attempt to interfere with the raiding party.

"Where's Reckharts?" Gill asked, scowling around the table and ready to end any attempt at rallying the crowd.

Nobody answered, but at least two of the party looked in the direction of the Big Man's upstairs office. A nod from Gill gave Ballinger his orders. Turning, the detective started across the room towards the stairs and two patrolmen followed on his heels.

Four of the bouncers moved to block the way to the

stairs, standing across it in a watchful, wary manner, their leader holding his pick handle in one big hand. Ballinger did not break his stride, but walked steadily towards the waiting men.

"I've a search warrant signed out all nice and legal, boys," he warned. "We don't want any of you for anything – yet."

His words caused three out of the four to back off and move away. However the fourth, his reputation at stake, stood firm. Being the head bouncer, he felt that he must make a better showing than the other three. In a silence that could almost be felt, the bouncer measured his distance. Something in Ballinger's steady approach unnerved the man. Never before had any prospective victim come walking straight at the bouncer in the face of his pick handle's threat. So he made his move a shade earlier than he might under other cirumstances.

Up swung the pick handle which had cracked more than one head. Ballinger jumped forward and his baton lashed out. Wood thudded home, smashing into the inside of the bouncer's raised right wrist. The force of the blow numbed the entire arm and the bouncer's fingers opened, allowing the pick handle to fall to the ground. Again the baton swung, colliding with the bouncer's bristle-covered jaw and tumbling him to the floor.

Ignoring the fallen bouncer, Ballinger sprang forward and ran up the stairs. Followed by the two patrolmen, he went along the passage and halted outside the door of Reckharts' office. Reaching down, Ballinger gripped and twisted the knob then shoved at the door. It held firm and he nodded to the patrolmen. Down went two shoulders and the door shook under the impact of almost four hundred pounds of brawny, muscular manhood. Twice more the patrolmen charged and finally the lock burst open.

Baton ready for use, Ballinger went through the door and into the office. He entered ready for trouble, but found none. One glance told him that the raid had come too late and the prime catch of all had slipped its meshes.

Wasting no time in futile complaints, Ballinger sprang from the room, past the two patrolmen and made for the stairs. Even as he saw the empty state of the room, Ballinger began to think where Reckharts might have gone. Recalling what the Yegg had said about making preparations for the future, Ballinger figured that Reckharts found an empty money-bag when he opened the safe. Which meant the Big Man would need to go to another source to gather the necessary wealth. There had been no record of any bank accounts in the books and Ballinger figured that Reckharts held the majority of his ill-gotten gains out-side Chicago. There would be a reserve of course, probably in the safe at Reckharts' Streeterville mansion. Which meant that he might still have a chance of laying hold of the Big Man if he hurried.

On seeing Ballinger return without Reckharts, the crowd realized for the first time that they stood without the Big Man's protective influence. Not until that mo-ment did some resistance arise. Several fights broke out as men with crimes on their consciences tried to escape.

Assigned to the task of arresting Reckharts, Ballinger did not intend to mix in the general mêlée which spread across the bar-room. However as he reached the foot of the stairs, he saw something which changed his mind. A patrolman, new to the business, had forgotten his training and committed the folly of looping the thong of his baton around his wrist instead of just over the thumb. Catching the end of the baton, one of the crowd twisted the thong so that it pinioned the officer's wrist in a painful manner. Although he wanted to get af-ter Reckharts, Ballinger knew he must help his fellow officer, for the rookie faced a serious injury. Jumping forward, Ballinger cracked the patrolman's attacker on the head and dropped him unconscious.

"Get that thong on right!" Ballinger ordered as the

patrolman's baton came free due to the collapse of his attacker.

Without another word, or even waiting to see whether his order was obeyed or not, Ballinger dashed across the room, passing in front of the bar on his way to the front door. Lighthouse, standing at the bar and gripping his bung-starter, watched Ballinger go by and a frown creased his face. Then a glow of realization came to the bartender's face as he became aware of where he had seen the Yegg's companion before. Discarding his original intention of joining the fight, Lighthouse dropped his pet weapon. He had seen his boss leave and guessed that Reckharts, knowing in some way of the approaching raid, made good his escape. There were no criminal charges against Lighthouse and a good bartender could always find employment, so he did not aim to jeopardize his chances by fighting and risking arrest for his actions.

Bursting through the batwing doors, Ballinger went to the uniformed lieutenant commanding the mounted detachment.

"Let me have a horse, Bill," he said. "I have to get after Reckharts."

"Take mine," was the reply. "Need any help?"

Reckharts tried to keep his social and business lives separate and his mansion's staff did not come from the criminal class. However the Big Man would not escape unless he took his bodyguard along. Knowing something of Mugs O'Toole, Ballinger decided that some help might be required.

"I only need one man," he said. "Somebody who knows the Streeterville district'd be best."

"Take Donovan," the lieutenant suggested, nodding to a burly elderly officer who sat a big, powerful horse.

Giving his long baton a cheery twirl, Donovan swung his horse alongside the bay which Ballinger mounted. Side by side, the two policemen rode away from the

Blue Boar and followed the direction taken earlier by Reckharts' cab.

In the saloon, swift action brought an end to the fight; although doing so took some time and caused a fair amount of damage. While the crowd outnumbered the raiding party, not all of its members joined in the fighting. Those who resisted did so under the disadvantage of knowing that a stiff jail sentence awaited any man who injured a police officer. So even the men who started to resist arrest soon gave up the attempt. Handcuffs were clipped on to wrists and the business of removing the catch to a more suitable location began.

"Cannon Baumer wants a word, sir," a patrolman said, saluting Gill as the chief of police stood with Mayor O'Bryan and Captain Mulrooney.

"Let's hear from him then," Gill replied, knowing that a number of the arrested men would be willing to sell out companions in an effort to curry the law's favor.

Baumer had never had any connection with the artillery side of the army, his nickname came from the underworld calling pickpockets 'cannons'. Coming forward, the head of Reckharts' pickpocket organization beamed ingratiatingly at the trio of men.

"Where's the Big Man, Cannon?" Bill asked.

"I dunno," Baumer answered. "Him and that Lash feller went upstairs."

"Who's Lash?" Mulrooney inquired, unable to place the man's name among Reckharts' regular associates.

"Is there anything for me if I help you?" Baumer countered.

"We'll see," promised Gill. "It depends on how much you help."

Knowing that Gill's word was his bond, Baumer went on with his attempt to shorten his forthcoming jail sentence.

"Lash's one of them Western gun-slingers we keep

hearing about. Come to town with the loot from a bank robbery. All in big bills that could be easy traced. So he brought them to the Big Man to get rid of them.''

"And did he get rid of them?'' Gill put in.

"I don't know. Him, the Big Man and Mugsy O'Toole went up to the office. It was early this morning. I'd come in for a drink before I went home and changed ready for the fight. Saw them going up. One of the bouncers had heard Lash and the Big Man talking and told me. Was just telling me when we heard a shot from upstairs. We all went up there fast, but the Big Man came out and told us that everything was all right. Only Mugsy's in Lake Michigan now.''

"Dead?'' asked O'Bryan in a startled tone.

"I've never seen anybody deader,'' Baumer replied. "Saw him when the boys brought him downstairs. There was this damned great hole between his eyes and it looked like somebody had burst open the back of his head from inside.''

"Did this Lash feller kill him?'' O'Bryan said, when neither of the policemen spoke.

"Couldn't say for sure,'' admitted Baumer. "All I know is, there were only three folks in the office. The Big Man never carried a gun, and Mugsy wasn't the kind to blow his own brains out.''

"What happened then?'' growled Gill.

"Lash started following the Big Man round like Mugsy used to. One way and another, Mugsy didn't object.''

"Hell's fire!'' Mulrooney spat out. "Frank's gone after Reckharts and he doesn't know about that feller Lash.''

Without another word, the detective turned and dashed across the room. He went through the crowd like it did not exist and burst out on to the street. Calling to the lieutenant in charge of the mounted officers, Mulrooney gave orders for six men to go after Ballinger. Knowing his lieutenant, Mulrooney did not need to ask where Ballinger had gone. All the burly captain knew was that he hoped the reinforcements arrived in time. Having once seen a Western-trained gun fighter in action, Mulrooney knew the danger into which Ballinger headed and guessed how little chance the lieutenant would have should what Baumer told him prove to be true.

Unaware of the danger into which he headed, Ballinger concentrated on getting the best possible speed out of his horse. Although a confirmed city-dweller, he had always enjoyed riding. A spell as a mounted officer did nothing to dispel his love of horses and he tried to spend at least a couple of hours every week in the saddle. So he found no difficulty in keeping up with Donovan. The patrolman, a light rider for all his build, knew the city like the back of his hand and had considerable experience in making good time through its streets.

Leaving the slum area of the Badlands behind, they wound through property which grew gradually better in quality and at last entered the exclusive area known as Streeterville. Reckharts' mansion stood in its own grounds, in a long street of similar dwellings. Evening was coming on and the street lay empty, only the occasional sight of a gardener working in the grounds of a house, or children playing on a spacious lawn gave any hint of life.

The big old colonial-style mansion bought by Reckharts' criminal activities stood silent, unlit and apparently deserted. Not until the two men drew rein at the ornate wrought iron gates did either speak.

"Reckon we can handle Mugs O'Toole between us, Mick?" asked Ballinger with a grin.

Sliding out the thirty-six-inch long baton from its boot on the saddle, Donovan grinned back. "I reckon we might at that, sir – happen we don't break a leg getting down from the saddle."

While riding for a couple of hours each week kept Ballinger in touch with horses, it did not retain the muscles needed for a long spell in the saddle and his body groaned in protest as he dismounted.

"It allus gets you," Donovan remarked, swinging down from his saddle and showing no sign of strain.

"I should get more time in, riding around one of the parks," Ballinger replied. "And will if I get a chance."

"They do say that you detectives work real hard," said Donovan dryly.

Ballinger had neither the time nor the inclination at that moment to become involved in the never-ending inter-departmental rivalry between the uniformed officers and the detectives. An old hand like Donovan, Ballinger's senior in service and far junior in rank, could be expected to regard the newly-formed Detective Bureau with amused contempt.

"We never stop working," Ballinger contented himself with replying, and secured the horse to the railings by the gate. "Let's go visit with Mr. Reckharts."

"The pleasure'll be all ours," answered Donovan.

Departmental differences were forgotten as the two men advanced along the path towards the house. Before they reached the building, they saw the front door open and Reckharts came out. A look of near panic came to the man's face and he halted, staring at Ballinger and Donovan.

"All right, Reckharts," Ballinger said. "We want you."

"And we mean to have you, darlin'," Donovan continued. "We can do it hard or easy. It all depends on you."

"Lash!" Reckharts screamed.

Hefting their batons, the two policemen started to move forward. They expected to see the huge shape of Mugs O'Toole burst out of the door and knew that he would take some handling. Little did Ballinger and Donovan know that O'Toole had met a man with the means and ability to render his bull's strength useless, that O'Toole had died early that morning, or that his killer was just behind Reckharts.

If either Ballinger or Donovan had time to think of anything when Lash came into sight, it may have been that Reckharts must be supported by the tall man as well as his regular bodyguard. However there was little time to think.

With something like a shock, Ballinger saw that the man before him held a long-barrelled Remington New Model Army revolver instead of the usual weapons the detective expected.

Landing with legs spread apart, knees slightly bent and body slanting forward, Lash did not trouble to raise the gun shoulder high and take sight. From waist high he fired. Flame flashed from the barrel of the gun and Ballinger halted in mid-stride as something smashed into him. Red hot fire knifed into his body and he felt himself flung backwards. His baton fell from a limp hand and blackness welled over him. Faintly, and growing fainter by the second, Ballinger heard Donovan's bellow of rage, then more shots but they seemed to be a long way off. Then everything went black.

CHAPTER SEVEN

The Fury of Two Women Scorned

Ed Ballinger stirred and opened his eyes. On trying to move, he felt a nagging ache in his side. For a moment his eyes saw only a milk-white blur, then the vision cleared and he looked around him. He realized that he lay in a bed and that Captain Mulrooney had risen from a chair to come forward. A puzzled frown came to Ballinger's face as he tried to decide why Mulrooney was in his bedroom. Only this was not his bedroom. Slowly Ballinger turned his head and studied his surroundings. He lay in a small, unfamiliar room. Flowers stood on a small table and a man wearing a white coat was watching him.

Then memory started to ebb back.

"Where's Reckharts?" he asked, trying to sit up and feeling something constricting his chest.

"Take it easy, Ed," Mulrooney ordered, laying a big but gentle hand on the other's shoulder and holding him down. "You've been hit bad."

Although Ballinger felt he should protest, shrug off the captain's hand, and rise, he could not do so. Somehow he had none of his usual strength. Also the nagging hurt in his side continued steadily.

"What happened?" he asked.

Seeing that Ballinger would not settle until he knew, the doctor nodded to Mulrooney.

"Reckharts got away after he shot you," the captain explained.

"How about Donovan?"

Before answering, Mulrooney glanced at the doctor and received another nod. "He's dead, Ed."

A low growl burst from Ballinger's lips. Everything came back to him in a single flash. He could almost see that tall, tanned man lunging forward, going into the crouching position, lifting and firing the gun. The other shots he heard as he fell must have been sent into Donovan.

Ballinger's head sank back on to the pillow. Poor old Donovan. A good, if not over-smart and brilliant, officer and a damned good man. He had been liked and respected by most people his duties brought him into contact with. Now he was dead, shot down without a chance. Maybe he had died the way he would wish, in the line of duty, but his killer had escaped.

"You'd best rest, Ed," Mulrooney said gently, knowing how the other must feel. "You're in poor shape yourself."

"But Reckharts—" Ballinger began.

"We've done all we can, but nothing's come up. Still, we've only been on it for two days."

"T - two days?"

"That was a bad wound you took, Ed. If I'd known earlier about Lash, I'd've sent more men along."

"Who's Lash?"

"The feller with Reckharts. He's a western gunfighter and outlaw. Killed Mugs O'Toole only that morning. Soon's I heard, I sent six men to help you but they got there too late. They found you lying in front of the house, damned near bled white and got you into the hospital as quickly as they could. You've been unconscious since then."

"And Reckharts got away," Ballinger said bitterly.

"He won't get far," answered Mulrooney, trying to

sound more certain than he felt knowing the difficulties which lay ahead.

In 1870 there was no system of inter-state communication, no radio networks to flash out messages of warning to alert other law enforcement officers, no central Federal agency such as the F.B.I. to act as a clearing house and gathering point of information. True the telegraph system had become reasonably well-developed, but it did not reach to every town and the sending of long, complicated messages, such as the descriptions of two fugitives, rarely proved satisfactory as there were too many elements which could go wrong. Even circulating reward posters through the mails took a very long time. With the whole of a vast country to disappear into, Reckharts stood a good chance of evading arrest.

"You've been here long enough, Captain Mulrooney," the doctor put in. "The lieutenant needs rest."

"Damn it, I'm all right now!" Ballinger objected, trying to sit up. "Where the hell're my clothes?"

"You couldn't walk a yard in your condition," the doctor said, calmly holding Ballinger down. "And rest easy or you'll burst open your wound."

"Go to hell!" Ballinger spat out, struggling against the man's hand.

Then a feeling of exhaustion ebbed over him. He lay back and stopped struggling. Nodding in satisfaction, the doctor signalled to Mulrooney and the captain left the room. Almost before the door closed, Ballinger had fallen asleep.

Two days passed by before Mulrooney returned to visit his wounded lieutenant. Sitting on the side of Ballinger's bed, the captain gave news of the latest developments, little as they were.

"Nothing on Reckharts and Lash yet," he said. "We did find out that Lash robbed a bank in Billings, Montana. At least, that's the only big robbery in recent months and a fair part of the loot was in large bills. Lash came here to get Reckharts to change them for him."

"You'll be short-handed," Ballinger remarked. "Maybe I should—"

"You'll stay in bed until the doc says you can get out, or I'll have a harness bull sit by it ready to knock you back with his night-stick," threatened Mulrooney. "I need you back real bad, Ed. But I need a whole, healthy man."

Although he hated to admit the idea, Ballinger knew that Mulrooney spoke the truth. He would be a liability, not an asset, if he tried to return to duty before fully recovered. However Ballinger could not relax. A man used to working ten to twenty hours a day when on a case found being bedridden tedious and boring.

"What's happened so far?" he asked.

"The officer in charge of the reinforcements I sent after you got off two of his crew to the railroad depot and docks as soon as he saw what had happened, but they didn't have any luck. Neither officer saw anything of Reckharts, although they both know him. As soon as I heard, I sent off telegraph messages along the track requesting all peace officers to keep watch for Reckharts and that Lash feller. So far nobody's seen them."

"How about the docks?"

"Nothing sailed on Saturday evening, and since then I've had every boat searched just before it left. Nothing there either."

Ballinger gave a low growl of anger and disappointment. After all the planning, with victory almost in their grasp, it seemed a little hard that the supreme prize should slip through the law's fingers. While the raid gathered in a prime selection of thieves and grafters, the organizing genius, the brains behind the whole affair, escaped. Of course he would never dare return to Chicago, but might – in fact was almost certain to –

start operations in some other area.

"Say!" Ballinger ejaculated. "He might still be hiding in town."

"It's possible," admitted Mulrooney. "But I doubt it. Not only are we after Reckharts, but there's a big reward offered for Lash. Pinkertons are after him and every informer knows there's good money to be made finding him. One way and another Reckharts hasn't many friends left in town. Especially since somebody started a rumor that the Big Man learned we were on to him and sold out the crowd at the Blue Boar to make sure he escaped."

"You wouldn't know how that rumor got started, would you, Cis?"

"*Me?* Sure and would I be doing such a mean, underhand thing as that, Ed?"

Despite his disappointment at losing Reckharts, Ballinger managed a grin. He knew how criminals thought and acted. Honor among thieves, loyalty to each other, was no more than a romantic writer's dream; few criminals trusted their kind. Enough of Reckharts' men would believe the rumor, because that was how they would act under the same conditions. With a desire for revenge, the deserted men might give away much the law could use. There were criminal hideouts in the city that not even the best informed stool-pigeon knew of. If Reckharts should be hiding in one, an angry, vengeance-seeking prisoner might mention it.

"If he got out of town, where would he go?" asked Ballinger. "I'd guess at New York, or Philadelphia. Reckharts is a big-city man."

"Lash isn't," Mulrooney pointed out.

"You reckon that he might have took Reckharts West with him?"

"Could be. But that covers a whole heap of ground."

"Sure; and most of it policed by dumb country-hick

lawmen,'' Ballinger groaned. ''There's no chance of getting help from them.''

''Maybe not,'' Mulrooney grunted, and hauled out his watch. ''I'll have to be on my way, Ed. The first of the trials starts tomorrow. Maybe we'll hear something soon.''

But the days went by and became weeks without the law receiving a single hint of where Reckharts had fled. Aided by rest, good doctoring, and an iron-tough physique, Ballinger recovered from his wound and returned to duty. Even though the breaking of Reckharts' organization disrupted much crime in the city, Ballinger found himself with plenty of work to do. Yet he never forgot the departed Big Man, or let up in his attempts to trace the other. On leaving the hospital, Ballinger visited every stool-pigeon he knew and passed word that he would pay well for information as to the Big Man's whereabouts. He questioned various members of the Reckharts' organization, visited the now almost recovered Sadie the Goat and Gallus Maggie in turn, but could learn nothing.

Then Ballinger picked up a whisper which gave him a fresh interest. The head bartender of the Blue Boar – sold by the city and now under new management – quit his job and disappeared. Not even his wife knew where Lighthouse might have gone, or if she did, held out against Ballinger's questioning. Other members of Reckharts' saloon bunch, who had no criminal charges against them, also faded from the scene and left no trace of their going.

Ballinger pressed on with his search, spending what time he could spare upon it and hoping against hope that something might turn up. Remembering his last meeting with Reckharts' new bodyguard, Ballinger practiced shooting. After a few attempts at copying the way Lash shot at him, Ballinger discarded the idea and put the wound he received down to pure luck on the other's part. Instead he concentrated on improving his aim. Burning countless bullets, he soon reached the point where he could stand on the line, raise his Smith and Wesson shoulder high, take aim and plant nine bullets out of ten into the bulls-eye of a target twenty-five yards away – a far higher standard than any other officer on the Chicago Police Department.

Almost a year went by and Ballinger was no nearer discovering the whereabouts of the Big Man. Then one afternoon—

"Hey, Lieutenant," said a voice as Ballinger strolled along the sidewalk in search of a safe-breaker badly wanted by the law.

Turning, Ballinger faced a member of the Pine Road Rollers who had slipped the net, through lack of evidence rather than innocence of offence, during the big clean-up. The man looked less affluent than in pre-clean-up days, but so did most of Chicago's criminal society.

"Well?" asked Ballinger.

"Gallus Maggie told me to find you. She says for you to meet her at the Gold Room in South State Street—"

"I know it," Ballinger interrupted. "What does she want with me?"

"Never said," the man replied. "Only to ask you to be there at three tomorrow afternoon."

"I'll think about it," Ballinger promised, and walked away.

Probably he would have done little more than think, but on his return to headquarters he found a further development awaiting him. After filling in the blotter, the official record of arrests and arrested persons, the desk sergeant ordered a patrolman to take Ballinger's safe-breaking prisoner to the cells, then grinned at the lieutenant.

"Allus thought you was a ladies' man, Ed," he said. Long service carried certain privileges such as using the first name when addressing one's superiors on an unofficial matter.

"Have I denied it?" answered Ballinger, wondering what the other was getting at.

"Had one of the East Stockyard boys in. Says that Sadie the Goat wants to see you at the Gold Room, that's on—"

"South State Street, they do tell me," growled Ballinger. "She wouldn't want me to be there at three tomorrow afternoon, would she?"

"You've been peeking," grunted the sergeant. "Now what do you think of that?"

"Thanks, Heimie," Ballinger said absently and turned to walk away.

"*Detectives!*" grunted the sergeant, and settled down to reread the newspaper interrupted by Ballinger's arrival.

On his way upstairs, Ballinger gave thought to this new and surprising development. He took the news to Mulrooney's office.

"Could be that they've found out who started the threats that caused the fight," Mulrooney warned.

"Could be," agreed Ballinger.

"Are you going?"

"I reckon I will. Don't figure they'd pick a place like the Gold Room to jump me, even if they knew. I've nothing to lose by going."

"Reckon not. Want for me to have a paddy-wagon standing by in the area?"

"I'll chance my luck without it," grinned Ballinger.

For all his levity, Ballinger took both his Smith and Wesson and billy along the following afternoon. He debated on carrying his pet baton in his pants pocket but decided that it might be superfluous. The Gold Room stood on the better end of South State Street and was a clean place which gave the law no trouble. Such a location would hardly be Sadie's and Maggie's choice if they aimed to take reprisals on him for his part in stirring up their savage and bloody fight.

Yet Ballinger could not imagine why they both asked him to be at the Gold Room. It might be nothing more than coincidence, but he doubted that. Especially as, on entering, he saw them seated together in one of the alcoves offered to such customers who did not wish to be in plain view.

Both Maggie and Sadie dressed fairly well, despite the curtailment of most of their more prosperous activities. A turban-like covering hid the fact that Sadie no longer had a left ear. Even when not wearing a hat, Maggie's hair covered the bare patch on the top of her skull. Although each carried marks, most of the visible signs of their fight had gone.

While crossing the room, Ballinger found himself struck by the friendly manner in which the two women sat talking. On seeing him approach, both gave warm and amiable smiles. They showed no animosity, so Ballinger wondered if something other than revenge on his person lay behind the invitation.

"Hi, Lieutenant," Maggie greeted. "Sit down."

"Have a drink," Sadie went on, not to be outdone in hospitality.

Taking a seat, Ballinger accepted the offered drink. He took the precaution of sniffing at the liquor, but could not detect the warning smell of butyl-chloride or any other noxious addition to the whisky.

"I never thought I'd find you pair sat here together like this," he remarked.

"We've called off our feud," Maggie explained.

"It should never have started," Sadie continued. "But we were tricked into fighting."

Slowly Ballinger lowered his hand to the pocket which held the billy. If either woman made a wrong move, he aimed to whip out the deadly, lead-loaded little persuader and swing. Sadie and Maggie knew too many dirty-fighting tricks for him to take chances with them, and he did not intend to be influenced by the fact that they were women.

"That's right, Ed," Maggie spat out. "We were tricked. Sadie never sent out any of those messages I got, and I for sure never said anything about her."

Which, while not exactly true, seemed to satisfy both girls.

"So who tricked you?" asked Ballinger, legs ready to thrust back his chair for a hurried rise to his feet.

"Can't you guess?" hissed Maggie.

"That dirty, double-dealing bastard, Reckharts, that's who!" Sadie snarled. "If we didn't send out those warnings, he must have. Lighthouse said later that the saloon took more that morning and afternoon before the law came than they did in three normal days."

"Which means that the Big Man, rot his guts, set us against each other so he could make a buck," Maggie continued. "And the dirty rat never gave us as much as a red cent or kind word after it was over."

"So how does all this affect me?" asked Ballinger, hoping against hope that the answer would give him something important.

"You're after him," Maggie stated. "Only you can't find him."

"We know where he is," Sadie finished.

Ballinger could hardly believe his ears or luck. Watching the women's faces, he could read no hint of trickery or deceit. Unless he was far wrong he could rely on them to tell him the truth. At long last he might discover the whereabouts of the Big Man.

Thinking of some of the things he heard in his travels around the city, Ballinger understood the women's attitudes and even guessed at the cause of their unexpected friendship. There had been a growing pressure from the East Stockyard boys that Sadie should demand a return engagement and attempt to regain her lost prestige by whipping Maggie. After losing an ear, Sadie showed some reluctance to risking another clash. While victorious in their meeting, Maggie knew that she did not grow any younger and next time might not see her so fortunate. So both women took steps to avoid another clash being forced on them. A truce was called and in the meeting each discovered that the other had not originated the threats and warnings which caused the fight. Maybe they did not believe each other, but sought for a scapegoat. Fortunately they decided that Reckharts possessed the best motive for making trouble.

"How'd you find out where he was?" asked Ballinger, trying to hide his excitement and eagerness.

"Through Lighthouse's wife," Sadie explained.

"But we questioned her and watched her for weeks," the detective objected.

Grins creased the two women's faces and Maggie replied, "You didn't watch her for long enough – or ask her the right way."

Which was true enough. Ballinger's men tried to watch the wife of the missing Lighthouse, but after a couple of weeks he had to take them off the assignment due to pressure of work.

"Maggie happened to mention seeing Becky, that's Lighthouse's wife," Sadie said. "All of a sudden Becky's dressing real well and spending like a drunken sailor. She'd been short of cash since he pulled out. So we had our boys watch her. A couple of days back, one of my boys followed her to the Wells Fargo office and saw her collect a letter. He dogged her to a hat shop and she bought a fancy chicken roost,* paid from a thick wad of notes. As soon as I heard, I collected Maggie and we paid Becky a little visit."

"She told us all we wanted to know," commented Maggie.

"Is she still in one piece?" growled Ballinger.

"Sure. We ruffled her feathers a mite, slapped her

---

* Chicken roost: Name given to the large-brimmed feather-decorated hats of the period.

around a bit – not much though. Then she told us where Lighthouse is.''

"Where, Maggie?" asked Ballinger.

"Working for the Big Man again.''

"Where?"

"Look, Ed, I'm leaving town. Was going before I learned about this,'' Maggie answered, the latter part clearly to lull any suspicions Sadie might feel. "Sadie's taking over my place and aims to go straight. Can you stop Becky making trouble over our visit?"

"I'll try,'' Ballinger promised, knowing the threat of arrest for withholding information would chill Becky's desire for revenge through the law.

"Lighthouse's working in Reckharts' saloon at Jack City. That's in John County, South Texas. The Big Man owns the saloon, a ranch and a fair piece of the town, Becky tells us.''

"Thanks, girls,'' Ballinger said, and reached towards his inside pocket.

"Forget it, Ed,'' Maggie stated.

"Sure,'' agreed Sadie. "All we want for you to do is get Reckharts – and stretch his lousy neck.''

CHAPTER EIGHT

Jack City Extends its Hospitality

While jolting over the last few miles of his journey to Jack City, Ballinger tried to make himself more comfortable in the swaying Conestoga stage coach which the Wells Fargo agent at Galveston swore was the latest thing in speed, style and delectation.

After extracting all the information possible from the two women, he had returned to headquarters and reported to Mulrooney. Being big-city policemen, they both had little but contempt for the small town lawmen one might expect in country districts and doubted if such men would be able to handle the arrest of a smart jasper like Reckharts without more experienced supervision. So it had been decided that Ballinger would go along, take up the Big Man and return with him to Chicago for trial. In his grip, Ballinger carried his pet baton and the necessary documents for the extradition. How he achieved the arrest had been left to his own discretion.

While waiting for orders to leave, Ballinger had begun to grow a beard. Having heavy whiskers, his efforts proved successful and he doubted if any of his old Chicago acquaintances now working in Texas would recognize him. He intended to pose as a travelling salesman while looking over the ground. He dressed accordingly in pearl-grey derby, check suit and sporting a fancy neck-tie.

Since his arrival in Texas, after going by train to New York, then taking a ship along the coast south to Galveston, Ballinger had begun to wonder if he might be biting off just a mite more than he could chew. Every man he saw in the Lone Star State, even at Galveston, wore at least one revolver on his person and did so without any hint of self-consciousness. However he took comfort in the thought that he carried his Smith and Wesson with him and knew how accurately he could use it. During the war, much to his disgust, Ballinger was called for service with the Provost Marshal's Department and never saw active service. He had seen the difficulty most men found in handling the .44 calibre Army Colt, Remington or other models of big revolvers issued by the Federal brass and doubted if the rebels would prove more adept. Not having any personal experience to guide him, he figured he ought to be able to hold his own in a gun fight, especially as he was now prepared for such an eventuality.

A glance out of the window showed that the coach had now entered the outskirts of Jack City. On either side of the trail a scattering of adobe buildings appeared, thrown up it seemed at the whim of the owner and without any regard for civic planning. Then, after a remarkably short time, the coach rolled into the main business section of the city. Here at least civic planning showed to some extent as the business premises stood in a rough line and a board sidewalk connected one to the next.

The coach's team came to a halt before an adobe building which proudly announced itself to be the Wells Fargo depot of Jack City, John County, Texas. Thrusting open the door, Ballinger levered himself from the coach and to the sidewalk. After looking first right and left along the length of the main street, and observing the open range which spread out so close to where he stood, he turned his eyes up to where the driver and guard sat on the coach's box.

"Is *this* Jack City?" he asked.

"Sure is," agreed the guard, laying aside his shotgun and reaching for Ballinger's grip. "Growed no end in the last six months."

Looking at the score or so business premises and maybe twice as many ordinary houses, Ballinger wondered how the city could ever have been any smaller.

"Where's the hotel?" he asked.

"Well now," grinned the driver. "Don't reckon as how the folks here heard you was coming, so they never got 'round to building one. Try Harte's Tumbleweed Saloon down there. He's got rooms to rent."

"Thanks," grunted the detective, catching the tossed-down grip. "I'll do just that. I'll leave my big bag here and send for it if I move in."

"If you don't, you'll be sage-henning under the sky," answered the driver. "Ain't but the Tumbleweed and Chiquita Rosa's place got rooms to rent. A man'd get plumb tuckered out sleeping at Rosa's, and it'd come heavy on the pocket."

"I don't get you," Ballinger said.

"When you get a bed at Rosa's, you don't go to it alone," explained the driver. "Don't they have that sort of place where you come from?"

"I'm too young to know," answered Ballinger. "And I'll send for the bag."

"It'll be here," promised the guard and turned his eyes to where the depot agent made an appearance at the office door. "See you've woke up then."

"This ain't Galveston. I do it all myself here," the agent answered. "Howdy, mister, staying long?"

"Until the next stage goes through," Ballinger answered. "Say, is there any law in Jack City?"

" 'Course there is!" yelped the agent indignantly. "We've got everything a city needs. Sheriff's office, town marshal's office, jail and city hall are all along the street a piece."

"All in that pint-sized adobe shack there," grunted the guard. "Only don't go disturbing the marshal none. He sleeps about this time to get up strength to sleep all night."

"Don't you pay him no never mind," protested the agent. "This's a nice li'l town."

"Yeah!" put in the driver. "And we want to get out of it. Come on, sign for your mail sack so's we can roll."

Taking his grip, Ballinger walked along the edge of the street. A few horses and a buckboard stood before various buildings. Apart from a rider entering town, the detective appeared to have the street to himself. After one glance at the approaching man, a cowhand of the sort one occasionally saw in the stockyards area, Ballinger turned his thoughts to how he should handle the situation. While not expecting a city the size of Chicago, he had thought to find himself in a fair-sized town where he could remain unnoticed while deciding how to make his arrest. Now it seemed that his choice of a haven must be in Reckharts' saloon – Maggie had told him the name of the Big Man's new establishment – or the local brothel. If Ballinger knew anything about Reckharts, he figured the other would have an interest in the cat-house as well as the saloon. From what the guard said, Ballinger could not expect much help from the local law.

The Tumbleweed Saloon towered a full story higher than the rest of the town's buildings, having a second floor. Built sturdily from a mixture of adobe and timber, it took up a fair piece of street frontage and hinted at luxury within. Glancing through one of the windows, Ballinger examined the big barroom. Although the furnishings and bar did not quite come up to the old Blue Boar's standards, the room did not look too bad. Various gambling games stood waiting to give players a "chance" of winning money, but at the moment were not in use. Only a few men lounged at the bar, as far as Ballinger could see, none of the Blue Boar employees were present.

So interested in his study had Ballinger been that he did not notice the sound of hooves drawing nearer.

"Sure is one fancy-looking place," said a friendly, drawling voice.

Turning, Ballinger looked at the speaker as he sat the low horned, double girthed saddle of a big, powerful, yellowish colored stallion. An equally fine-made, saddled horse, this time a light bay, stood riderless at the side of the stallion, its reins secured to the other's saddlehorn. Being a city dweller, the horses meant little to Ballinger, although he noticed the coiled rope on the yellow animal's saddlehorn and the Spencer carbine in the boot. He studied the rider with a policeman's quick, careful eyes.

Young, six-foot odd in height, with a good, strong build. A low crowned, wide-brimmed Stetson hat sat on the back of the head, exposing a mop of unruly, fiery red hair and a cheery, tanned, freckled, pugnaciously handsome face. A tight rolled bandana of garish colors trailed long ends over his blue shirt. Brown levis pants hung outside his high-heeled, fancy stitched, spur-decorated boots, their cuffs turned back a good three inches. Around his waist hung a gunbelt, two walnut handled Army Colts butt forwards in the open topped holsters.

Swinging from his saddle, the cowhand looped both horses' reins over the hitching rail and stepped on to the sidewalk, halting to study the imposing front of the Tumbleweed again.

"Yes, sir!" he stated. "Real fancy. There's nothing like it in all of five hundred miles."

"You've rid *that* far?" asked Ballinger.

"Shucks no. Come down from the Rio Hondo country. Heard tell how Jack City's grown and came to see for myself. Name's Red Blaze, friend. If you're going in, I'll set up the drinks. Hate drinking alone, unless there's nobody to drink with.''

For a moment Ballinger studied the young man, wondering if he might be a tout employed by the management to steer customers into the saloon. It seemed to be hardly likely. That tanned face did not look to belong to such a cheap game, although Ballinger knew that looks could prove deceptive. Yet such a fancy place would hardly need to employ touts as a means of drawing trade. If Ballinger knew anything about cowhands – and his occasional meetings with the breed in Chicago led him to believe he did – the Tumbleweed would draw them like iron to a magnet.

''Be pleased to,'' he said. ''The name's Ed Farrel. I sell shaving and washing soap.''

''You've come to a bad place to try,'' Red commented. ''Let's see if the drinks are as fancy as the place looks.''

Thrusting open the batwing doors, Red led the way into the room. Even as the men walked towards the bar, a couple of girls came to join them.

''Hi, handsome,'' the blonde of the pair greeted. ''Would you see a couple of gals die of thirst?''

''I surely never have yet,'' answered Red. ''What'll it be?''

''There's some here who drink beer,'' answered the brunette. ''But if you can only run to that, we'd best call them.''

''Just back from a trail drive, gal,'' boomed Red. ''I'm loaded for beer and my *amigo* owns his own factory back East. We're not beer-drinking men. Hey, Colonel, set up wine for the ladies and drinks for us.''

''Sure thing, sport,'' agreed the bartender.

Watching the young cowhand flash a fair-sized roll of money, Ballinger felt tempted to give out with some sage advice. More alert than his new companion,

Ballinger saw how the bartender and girls eyed the money and caught the exchange of glances between the saloon's employees.

The girls gave Ballinger no time to think how he might save the rash young cowhand's bankroll without exposing himself. Hanging on to Red's arms they began to dazzle him with smiles. The bartender wasted no time either, but produced "wine" for the ladies and then brought out a bottle bearing the label of a nationally famous distillery.

"Nothing but the best, gents," he said, deftly extracting the cork and pouring out two stiff drinks.

"Wowee!" Red ejaculated, after tasting his drink. "That sure came out of the right bottle."

In a way Ballinger agreed with his companion. He had drunk the same brand of whisky in Chicago, yet it tasted different there. Sipping again, Ballinger wondered at the raw taste, yet it held no hint of the usual doctoring some places gave to their drinks to make the original supply go further than its maker intended.

"Should be," the bartender answered, filling the glasses again. "The boss fetches it all the way from the distillery in St. Louis."

"He must be tired after the trip," Ballinger said.

"Huh?" grunted the bartender.

"Carrying it all that way."

"Carry – oh, sure," the bartender replied, then burst into forced laughter as might be expected of one in his position when a paying customer made even a bad joke. "That's good."

"You should tell it to him," Ballinger stated. "Is he here?"

"Who?"

"The boss."

"Naw. He's out at his ranch. You wanting to see him?"

"Sure. My company's running a new line in shaving soap. Mounting it in a whisky glass. Thought that saloons might like to buy some for passing out to the customers.''

"I wouldn't know about that. You'd have to ask the house manager. Only he ain't here right now either."

"Come on, Ed," Red put in. "You leave the business until later. Right now we've got some drinking—" He paused and grinned rakishly at the girls, "and things, to do."

"You *are* the one," the blonde simpered. "Hey, my feet hurt, let's sit at a table, shall we?"

"Sure," agreed Red. "Take the bottle, girls. How's about you toting ours, Ed. I'll just buy another couple to take back for the boys at the O.D. Connected."

Having learned that Reckharts was not in town, Ballinger decided that he would stay with the cowhand and try to save the other from being taken for every cent in his pocket. Accordingly he picked up the bottle and his glass, preparing to follow the girls to one of the tables. Red bought another two bottles of the whisky and carried them triumphantly to join the rest of the party.

On sitting down, Ballinger looked around him with some interest. Business appeared to be slack for the majority of the occupants of the saloon looked to be employees of one kind or another waiting to start work, or resting between shifts. An old swamper wandered about the room, making ineffectual dabs about him with a sweeping brush.

From the start it became clear that the girls did not intend that Red take any money out of the room with him. Sipping the colored water which passed as wine in their set, they continued to dazzle the cowhand with their conversation. Clearly the girls accepted Ballinger's pose as a travelling salesman and regarded him as an interloper trying to cut in and get free drinks from their victim.

"Say, Red," the blonde remarked. "Do you feel like making some money?"

"I always do," Red agreed, looking owlish and

slightly drunk despite only taking two drinks. "Runs in the family. Uncle of mine made him a fortune crossing talking parrots with golden eagles."

"What did he get?" gasped the brunette.

"Damned if I know, gal," Red admitted. "But when them crosses talked, it sure paid a man to listen."

The girls laughed, then the blonde suggested that Red tried to make his fortune in an easier way.

"Why not try your hand at bucking the tiger?" she went on, nodding to the faro layout nearby.

"Don't like tigers, they bite," Red answered. "Can't say I go for them spinning cages neither, the dice rattling remind me of diamond-backs."

It became apparent that none of the saloon's gambling games appealed to the young man. Ballinger felt relieved for he guessed that there would be very little chance of the house losing at any of the offered games.

A short, thin, sly-looking man approached the table. Clad in loud city clothing, the man was a type Ballinger knew all too well and could even guess at the newcomer's line of work. Sure enough, the man produced three empty half walnut shells and a dried pea.

"Come to get some of the money back that you gals have won off me," he declared, setting the pea on the table and covering it with one of the shells. "Are you going to give me a chance?"

"He almost never wins," the blonde told Red in a stage whisper, while her friend agreed to give the newcomer a chance to win back some of the money taken from him in earlier games.

Drawing up her skirt's hem and exposing a shapely, black stocking-clad leg, the brunette extracted some money from under her garter. She laid a five-dollar bill on the table, studied the shells as the man rapidly shifted their positions, then pointed to the one on the right.

"This one?" grinned the operator, then his face lost the smile as the pea appeared. "Damn it, Mame, you win again."

"Let me have a try," the blonde suggested.

Once again the ritual of placing the pea in position and moving the shells began. After a series of fast moves, the man allowed the blonde to make her selection. On losing to the blonde, the man paid her from a fat bundle of notes. Then Red said just what Ballinger feared he would.

"Hey, that's quite a game, friend," the cowhand enthused.

"How about a drink on me, Red?" Ballinger put in, hoping to create a diversion and save the young man's money.

"Shucks, there'll be no need for us to pay for our liquor. This gent here'll do it," Red answered. "Go to it, friend. I'll lay me five dollars that I can guess that old pea right out for you."

"Hey, Ed," Mame put in, before Ballinger could say another word. "Do you sell any of that fancy-smelling soap for ladies?"

"Huh?" grunted Ballinger, then remembered his pose. "Sure I do. Say, why don't we all go down to the stage depot and I'll give you samples out of my bag."

"Let's see Red win some money first," she countered.

However Red did not win. Although he concentrated with savage intensity on the moving shells, the pea proved to be under one that he did not choose.

"Takes real quick eyes to win," the operator of the game announced and started to put away his shells.

"I just wasn't looking right," Red replied indignantly. "Let's give her another whirl."

"If you double your bet and win, you'll get back the money you lost last time, Red," the blonde whispered.

"Why sure," he agreed, beaming at such an easy answer to his problem. "You set a limit on this here game, friend?"

"If you reach the roof, we'll take if off," the man answered. "Come on, the hand is quicker than the eye, or is it? Here they go and the pea is under the shell in the middle – or is it?''

"Under the shell on the left," Red guessed.

Raising the cowhand's selection, the man showed that the pea did not lie beneath it.

"You can't lose three times in a row, Red," the blonde insisted. "And if you double up again, you'll still show a profit."

Watching the old shell game in operation, Ballinger found himself torn between his desire to save the young cowhand's money and do his duty. To interfere would make him mighty unpopular in the saloon and spoil his chances of staying in Jack City while planning his campaign against Reckharts. Yet he hated to sit idly by while that friendly young cowhand, who appeared to be drunk on the small amount of whisky taken so far, was robbed by an ancient swindle no ten-year-old city boy would fall for.

Again Red doubled his bet and the ritual ran its course. After shuffling the shells, the operator looked up and grinned at his victim.

"Go to it, cowboy. This time you're sure to win."

"I'll take the middle one," Red answered. But, before the other could move, reached out and raised the two flanking shells. "No pea under either of them. It must be with the one I picked."

A signal from the operator started a pair of brawny, obvious bouncers moving towards the table. Anger creased his face as he glared at the smiling Texan.

"That's not how the game's played," he objected.

"Mister," Red replied. "That's how I play it."

Only his voice sounded different. At the same instant Ballinger, the operator of the shell game and the two saloon girls realized that the young cowhand was cold sober.

CHAPTER NINE

Jack City Speeds its Departing Guests

While the people at the table became aware of Red Blaze's sobriety, the bouncers failed to notice any change. So neither man took any special care, believing that they had only the usual half-drunk cowhand to handle. It proved to be a painful and disastrous mistake.

Big arms reached out to enfold Red from the rear and hold him until the second bouncer rendered him incapable of argument. Watching in the bar mirror's reflection, Red saw his danger and handled it. Back drove his right elbow to smash with considerable force into the reaching man's solar plexus. Letting out a strangled grunt of agony, the man made a hurried retreat. On the heels of dealing with his first assailant, Red pivoted and whipped a backhand swing around to take the second bouncer squarely on the nose. Such a blow was painful in the extreme and the man went staggering backwards, blood spurting from his pulped nasal organ.

Letting out a squeal of unlady-like curses, Mame grabbed at the neck of one of the bottles. Red laid a hand in the centre of her face as she started to rise and shoved hard. Curses became a wail of despair as the girl's chair tipped over and deposited her, in a flurry of skirts and waving legs, on the floor.

Other members of the saloon staff started coming

into the attack. The shell game operator grabbed at his jacket pocket, while some eight men swarmed forward. Ballinger acted almost without conscious thought. Out lashed his fist, colliding with the jaw of the shell game man before his fingers gripped the butt of the Derringer in his pocket, and shooting him to one side.

Once committed, Ballinger knew he must fight and also that bare hands could not offset the extra numbers of the opposition. Salvation loomed to one side and the detective took steps to obtain it. Jumping to where the swamper stood and stared, Ballinger snatched the brush from unresisting hands. A kick tore off the bristled head and left almost a facsimile of the thirty-six-inch long baton Ballinger had carried when a mounted policeman and still used when occasion demanded one's extra length.

Holding his improvised baton, Ballinger swung to face his first attacker. Having bounded the bar in traditional manner, the bartender charged to the attack with bung-starter in hand. Knowing that such a weapon could cave in his head, Ballinger determined to keep its wielder at a distance. Throwing up the baton, the detective lunged one-handed almost as if handling an *épée de combat*. Unable to stop himself, the bartender rushed straight into the unyielding end of the baton. It caught him in the face with enough force to throw his co-ordination out of kilter. Ballinger gave the man no chance to recover. Taking hold of the baton with his other hand, he side-stepped the half-blinded bartender's rush and brought off a butt stroke which crashed the end of the baton into the side of the man's jaw.

Much as he enjoyed a good fight, and despite being a mite busy on his own account, Red Blaze found pleasure in witnessing as fine a display of the art of wielding a long baton as he would ever see. In Ballinger's hands the brush handle took on a new and, to his attackers, alarming life. Now its end thrust painfully into a belly, face or other tender spot; next, gripped in both hands, it parried a blow and delivered a staggering reply with end or centre; or it hooked under a kicking leg, heaved upwards and threw its victim over backwards; all in all Ballinger handled more than his end of the fight.

Not that Red did badly, considering he relied only upon his hands, elbows, knees and feet. Clearly he had learned how to fight from a very good teacher and could take punishment as well as hand it out. The attacking saloon workers found that they had caught a tiger but could not release it.

Mame came to her feet. Anger made her decide against following her fellow workers to safety. Instead she gave an enraged screech and started towards the main doors with the intention of calling for assistance.

"Stop her, Ed!" Red yelled, realizing what the girl intended to do and knowing the danger.

Whipping his baton across the side of a bouncer's head and knocking the man staggering, Ballinger brought it down and lunged. He thrust the wood between Mame's legs, tripping her and sending her once more to the floor. On withdrawing the baton, he found himself in trouble.

One of the attackers sprang forward and grabbed hold of the end of the pain-delivering baton, trying to tear it from Ballinger's grasp. While the detective knew how to handle such a situation, he doubted if he would be given time unless something happened.

It happened. Seeing Ballinger's predicament, Red knocked aside a gambler with whom he had been trading punches. Pivoting, the cowhand delivered a kick to one of the bouncers and landed it in an area guaranteed to make the man lose all hostile desires for some time. With the way momentarily cleared, Red sprang forward. Out shot his right hand, catching the collar of the bartender as he prepared to jump Ballinger. With a heave which ripped the man's shirt, Red pitched him aside. A hard left caught another attacker in the face and the pause gave Ballinger all the chance he needed.

The man had now a double hand hold on Ballinger's
stick. Stepping forward a pace, Ballinger laid hold with
his other hand between his assailant's. With a twisting
heave, exerting his full strength, Ballinger raised the
baton and tore it from the other's hands. In doing so,
Ballinger carried the baton into a raised position ideally
suited to delivering a butt smash at his attacker. Down
drove the baton, its end macing into the side of the
man's throat and tumbling him backwards with difficulty in breathing.

Having more experience of Western-style brawls than
the detective, Red knew that the time had come for
departure. Any moment now one of the saloon employees would forget about his desire to beat the men
into a pulp and reach for a gun.

Before the cowhand could yell a warning to leave,
Ballinger saw one of the room's interior doors burst
open. Lighthouse sprang through the door, a long
barrelled Army Colt in his right hand. From his appearance, Lighthouse had come up in the world, and
also had been enjoying either a sleep or female company
in the back room. He wore a fancy vest, frilly-bosomed
shirt without a collar and unbuttoned, while his elegant
white trousers showed signs of being hurriedly fastened.

"What the—" Lighthouse began, then his eyes met
the detective's and recognition flared in them. Beard or
no beard, Lighthouse knew Ballinger and remembered
what his previous failure to identify the detective had
cost. Starting to raise the Colt, he snarled, "Bal—"

Unfortunately for Lighthouse, Ballinger recognized
his old acquaintance even more quickly. Being close to
the table where the girls entertained Red and himself,
Ballinger had an ideal answer to Lighthouse. He
released the baton with one hand, caught up and hurled
a whiskey bottle across the room. For a snap shot, his
aim proved remarkably good. Caught in the belly by the
flying bottle, Lighthouse gave a croaking grunt,
doubled over and sank to his knees winded.

"Don't throw the other one!" Red yelled. "Grab it and let's get the hell out of here."

So saying, the cowhand ducked, caught a charging attacker around the knees, rose and pitched him over. Twisting around, Red leapt to the table and grabbed Ballinger's grip from the side of the detective's vacated chair. Another man lunged in Red's direction. Swinging up the grip, Red smashed it under the man's chin and knocked him sprawling.

Hurling his baton in a spinning arc so it struck a man who tried to draw a gun, Ballinger laid hold of the second full bottle of whisky and followed Red in a dash to the batwing doors. The saloon crew, such as might have prevented the departure, made no attempt to do so. Beating up customers was a pleasant change from the boring routine of work, but not when the customers showed such a strenuous, painful and determined objection to having the shape of their features altered.

"Can you ride?" asked Red, as they burst through the doors and on to the sidewalk.

"Sure," Ballinger answered.

"Then grab my bay and we'll put some distance between us and here."

"What about the local law?"

A shot cracked along the street and for the first time Ballinger heard the vicious "whap!" sound of a close-passing bullet. Looking along the street, he saw a trio of men leaping from a building some distance away. He noticed that all of the trio wore badges of office, although none sported any kind of uniform, and carried guns. Smoke still dribbled up from the barrel of the leader's weapon.

"That," said Red dryly, "is the local law. They work for the house."

Another shot ripped through the air close to Ballinger. Already Red was tearing free the two horses' reins. Although amazed at the thought of lawmen just shooting without so much as a challenge or discovering what had happened, Ballinger wasted no time in joining the cowhand.

"Did you bring the bottle?" Red whooped, going into his horse's saddle with a bound and still holding Ballinger's grip in his left hand.

"This's a helluva time to want a drink," the detective answered, hooking a foot into the restive bay's stirrup iron and mounting despite the difficulty when holding the whisky bottle in one hand.

Again lead buzzed by their heads, coming closer than the previous shots. Red hooked the handle of the grip over his saddlehorn. Twisting his right hand palm out, he drew the offside Colt. He threw a shot in the direction of the approaching men, kicking up a spurt of trail dirt ahead of them. By that time Ballinger had mounted the bay and Red wasted no more time.

"Let's go!" Red whooped, and started the yellow horse running.

Without waiting for any instructions from its rider, the bay followed. Only for a moment did Ballinger find any difficulty. While the range rig he sat differed in some respects from the McClellan pattern used by the mounted officers of the Chicago Police Department – copied from the U.S. Army saddle – Ballinger soon had its feel and gained control of his mount. More shots hummed by, but as the distance separating them from the town law increased, so the chances of being hit lessened.

"I'd've thought that Harte'd have better stock than that handling the law," Red yelled as they thundered by the Wells Fargo depot.

He did not know just how lucky they had been. Only three of the lesser lights in the marshal's office had been present when word of the fight arrived; its more prominent members being absent on other business. While taking pay for their knowledge of firearms rather than ability as law enforcement officers, none of the trio could be termed real good shots.

"You sound like you expected trouble," Ballinger answered.

"Like Cousin Dusty says," Red replied, "a man who expects trouble's ready for it. We'll stop once we're clear of town so I can put that bottle some place safe."

Swinging their horses from the trail, after passing the last of Jack's City's buildings, Red and Ballinger rode to the top of a slope. There the young cowhand halted his horse and dropped from the saddle. He opened a saddle-pouch and took out some rags.

"Don't they sell whisky where you live?" asked Ballinger, watching the careful way in which Red wrapped up the bottle before placing it into the pouch.

"Not like this kind," Red answered. "I'm sure pleased that you brought it out, Ed. Getting another bottle from the Tumbleweed wouldn't be so easy for me now."

A puzzled frown came to Ballinger's face. Clearly the cowhand had ridden a considerable distance for the purpose of buying the whisky. Yet it was a nationally known brand which ought to be easily obtainable in any town. Ballinger wondered what made the type sold in Reckharts' Jack City saloon so special. Before he could phrase the question, an interruption came.

"Just what makes it so spec—"he began.

"Let's ride," Red cut in, looking towards the town." They're coming to speed the departing guests."

Following the direction of his companion's glance, Ballinger saw several riders leaving town and heading in their direction. Yells rose as the approaching party realized that they had been observed and one jerked out a rifle. Although he fired a shot, the bullet came nowhere near Ballinger and Red

Vaulting his horse, Red led the way across the range astride and in a looping circle around the town. He did not make for the trail along which he entered Jack City, but kept his horse running across the open range. It soon became obvious that, while the pursuing party

aimed to continue the chase, none rode a horse capable
of out-running either the stallion or the bay.

"Going to have to lose 'em though," Red stated,
when Ballinger remarked on the matter. "And without
tuckering the horses too much. We've a long ride to
Polveroso and I hadn't figured on taking company back
with me."

While admiring the desirability of losing their pursuers, Ballinger could not see any chance of doing so out
in the open, rolling range country. In a city – a *real* city
not a pretentiously-named hamlet – he could have lost
anybody who tried to trail him; but out on the plains
there were no stores into which one could dash and slip
out through another entrance, no alleys down which a
man might dart and lose the follower; none of the things
he regarded as indispensable for the business of shaking
a tail.

If Red felt any concern over the lack of amenities, he
failed to show it. With considerable skill, he gauged the
pace of the horses so that the posse could not close the
distance; yet also retained a reserve of speed in case of
an emergency. Due to his training as a mounted
policeman, Ballinger fancied himself as a better than
fair horseman, but he soon found that his young companion was his master in the equestrian arts. Of course
Red, like almost every Texan, had been riding almost
since old enough to walk. In Texas a horse offered more
than a mere means of transport, it was a way of life and
a necessity for survival.

Over the range they rode, with Red picking as difficult a route as possible and choosing country which
would delay a larger body of men. Ballinger found his
riding skill put to a severe test, but managed to stay with
the redhead and not slow Red down in any way.

"Didn't think to ask," Red called after they had
covered almost two miles without losing their pursuers.
"Can you take a horse over a jump?"

"Sure."

"*Bueno*. That bay's a jumping fool."

The reason for the question became suddenly, shockingly, apparent as they rode up and topped a fold in the rolling range land. Another wide, open valley lay before them. At the foot of the gentle slope, out in the centre of the level bottom of the valley, a gash slit open the land; a gap at least thirty feet wide and with sheer, rocky walls. With horror, Ballinger realized that Red intended to make the horses jump that gap. Unless he intended to make a long detour, any other kind of crossing would be impossible for the gap split the bottom of the valley as far as the eye could see in either direction.

"We're going over *there*?" asked Ballinger.

"There's no place a man can ride down and up in four miles," Red answered, keeping his horse moving. "Like I said, the bay's a jumping fool. You've only two things to do. One's sit back, follow me and give him his head."

"And what's the other?"

"Make sure you land on the other side. Falling down that canyon wouldn't hurt you, but hitting the bottom'd be rough."

With that sage advice, Red started his horse moving and led the way down the slope. Ballinger allowed Red to draw ahead, not through fear of making the jump or lack of faith in his companion, but so as to see how the other handled it. While following Red down the slope, Ballinger studied the gap over which he must leap a strange, unfamiliar horse. Carved by the action of running water, the gap fell away sheer and deep but its rim appeared to be solid and capable of offering a firm footing for the horses.

Settling himself in the saddle, guiding the yellow stallion with strong, confident hands, Red headed it for the edge of the gap. Up and out sailed the horse then its steel-shod hooves struck solid ground. Red kept the horse moving for some yards beyond the edge, then turned it so as to see how Ballinger made the jump.

Never had the detective concentrated on anything as he did on measuring the distance to the edge of the gap. He was alert for the first hint that his mount would not jump, but felt nothing. On thundered the bay, picking up speed but still under complete control. Nearer and nearer rushed the gap. A touch with the heels, a gentle hint from the reins, and Ballinger felt the horse gather itself. Then it launched its body forward into space. Down below, looking far deeper than its twenty feet drop, water sparkled. It would not be deep enough to break his fall and save him from injury should the horse fail to reach the other side.

With what seemed like amazing slowness, the bay leapt over the gap, but the landing did not go off smoothly. Whatever the reason, the bay touched down and stumbled badly. Ballinger felt the horse going and left the saddle in a bound.

Red rode towards Ballinger as soon as he saw what had happened. Before the cowhand arrived, Ballinger – still holding the bay's reins – had approached the animal and bent to examine the foreleg it refused to put on the ground.

During the ride to the gap, Red had studied his companion and gauged his ability before attempting the dangerous jump across the gap. Nothing he had seen caused him to doubt that the other could make the leap. Only bad luck prevented Ballinger from making a perfect landing. Real bad luck with that Jack City bunch coming up fast.

"Get on and ride him up over the rim there, Ed," Red said, hating himself for having to make such a callous suggestion.

"Like hell!" Ballinger replied. "I'll walk up, or fight them off from here. But I'm damned if I'll ride a lame horse."

While Red could admire the other's sentiments—it

made a pleasant change to meet a dude who cared for a horse's welfare – he saw one difficulty in Ballinger carrying out one part of his idea. As far as Red could see, the other did not wear a gun. Making a fight against the Jack City posse under *that* advantage would be more suicidal than possible.

Even as the posse topped the opposite rim, Red jerked the Spencer carbine from his saddle boot, drew back the big side-hammer and threw the weapon to his shoulder. He did not intend to injure any of the posse unless forced, but aimed to warn them off. Knowing the inaccurate nature of his weapon, he did not attempt any fancy shooting. Instead, he concentrated himself with planting a bullet ahead of the men. It served the purpose and brought the posse to a halt. Clearly they expected more serious resistance, for they withdrew over the rim.

"Get going, Ed," Red ordered. "I don't know what sort of rifles they have with 'em, so let us not take fool chances."

Ballinger did not argue. Taking the bay's reins, he walked up the slope. Behind the departing detective, Red worked the Spencer's lever and replaced the used round with a loaded bullet. A rifle cracked from across the valley, its bullet cutting the air by Red's head. With something like relief, he noted that the sound of the shot did not carry the deep power of a Sharps or Remington buffalo rifle – weapons guaranteed to hold true at ranges of half a mile in competent hands. The posseman used a Winchester, which possessed about the same accuracy potential as his Spencer.

Turning, Red saw that Ballinger was half-way up the slope so he mounted his horse and followed. Once over the rim and clear of flying lead, Red dismounted and joined the detective in examining the bay's injured leg.

"It'll mend," Red guessed. "Only there'll be no riding him for a spell." He returned to the rim and looked back to where the posse had ridden down to the gap. "I figured none of them would chance it," he continued, rejoining Ballinger. "If we don't rush, my clay-bank'll carry double."

For the first time Ballinger learned the name Texans gave to horses of that yellowish mixture of sorrel and dun color.

"There's no need for that," he answered. "I walked a be – I'll walk and lead the bay. It won't be much slower than riding double."

"They're your aching feet," grinned Red, growing to respect the other more with each show of concern for the welfare of the horses. "We'll head down towards the stage trail. Happen we're lucky, we'll pick up a range-grazer, or meet somebody on the trail who'll lend us a horse."

"How about our friends from Jack City?" asked Ballinger.

"Reckon we've seen the last of them," Red replied. "If I know their kind, they won't work too hard to catch up with us now we've crossed the canyon. It'd be too much like work to go around it and find us again."

CHAPTER TEN

Jack City Resumes its Attentions

Night came without any sign of a horse left out on the range to graze and without meeting a person who could loan a mount. In the hope that one or the other might appear, Red and Ballinger stuck to the stage trail. But they pushed on at the best possible speed, for Red wished to reach Pronghorn Springs before dark.

At last, with the sun sinking in the west, Ballinger saw a small lake ahead of them. Much to his surprise, he noticed a stack of cut wood piled by the side of the trail not far from the lake. Then he realized that it must be left there by the Wells Fargo Company for the use of any coach which found itself halted for the night and unable to reach Jack City.

Before settling down to making camp, Red rose to his feet and stood on the back of his horse. From that vantage point he studied their backtrail, searching it for any sign of pursuit.

"Like I thought," he said. "There's nobody after us."

"May as well throw up our camp then," Ballinger answered.

"Reckon so," agreed Red, dropping to the ground. "I hadn't expected to be away for so long, so I didn't bring any food along."

Wanting to know a few things about his companion,

Ballinger remarked. "We've that bottle of whisky with us."

"I never like drinking outside a saloon," Red answered. "As soon as we've tended to the horses, if you'll make a fire, I'll see if I can raise us some supper."

Ballinger nodded and went to the bay. After removing the horse's saddle and laying it on its side by the trail, Ballinger watched Red stroll away from the camp. He had noticed the care the cowhand showed in putting down the saddle and felt even more curious about Red's reason for bringing the bottle of whisky. Then Ballinger found something else to interest him. Instead of taking the Spencer carbine, Red drew his right-side Colt and carried the handgun ready for use.

Not far from the camp, a large jack rabbit bounded from cover and shot away as fast as it could go. Instantly Red flopped forward, landing belly down on the ground. With both elbows dug firmly in the grass, Red supported his right hand with the left and took sight. He did not attempt to fire at the speeding rabbit, but after covering about fifty yards it did what he expected. Halting, the rabbit turned and sat up to look back. Making sure of his aim, Red squeezed the Colt's trigger.

Standing watching, Ballinger heard the flat bark of the Colt and saw the rabbit bounce into the air then flop on to its side. He gave a low whistle of admiration for he had not expected the other to make a hit at such a long range.

"That was good shooting," he complimented, as Red returned carrying the now headless jack rabbit. "If it'd been me, I'd have taken the Spencer."

"So'd I, if there'd been a chance of something bigger'n a jack," Red replied. "Trouble being that if you hit a jack with a Spencer, you hit him all over. Saves skinning him out, but sure spreads the meat around."

Deftly the cowhand skinned his trophy and prepared to cook it. Later on he and Ballinger sat in the darkness by the fire. Although eaten with the fingers and without the benefit of vegetables or even salt, Ballinger found the rabbit's meat palatable and satisfied some of the pangs of hunger he felt. With the meal over, the detective tried to satisfy his curiosity.

"Why'd you want the whisky so bad?" he asked.

"Like I said, you don't see much like it."

"I've seen Dennison's Old Whipping Post on sale in plenty of places."

"Not like this kind," Red answered, nodding to his saddlepouch. "Say, did you leave anything in town?"

Clearly he did not intend to go any further in the matter of his purchase and Ballinger knew enough about interrogation to call off his attempt. He wondered if he should show Red the identity wallet but decided against doing so until he knew more about the other.

"Only my bag, down at the Wells Fargo office," he replied. "Reckon I've lost that now."

"I wouldn't say that," Red drawled. "Even in Jack City they'd fight shy of robbing property on Wells Fargo land. When we get to Polveroso, I'll round up a few of the boys and we'll go collect the bag for you. Sure hope Cousin Dusty's home though."

"Cousin Dusty?"

"Likely you've heard of him. Dusty Fog."

"I've heard," agreed Ballinger.

Any man who associated with Texans even briefly could hardly avoid hearing about the man called Dusty Fog. Ballinger wondered how many of the stories he had heard from visiting cattlemen might be true. Among other things, they claimed that Dusty Fog rode as a Confederate Army captain at seventeen and built a name as a fighting cavalry leader equal to Dixie's Mosby and Turner Ashby; how he now acted as segundo, foreman, of one of Texas' biggest ranches and was a trail boss equal in ability to the best. After the end of the war, if the Texans told true, Dusty Fog handled a real

important national matter in Mexico.* He was said to
have brought law to a Montana mining town where
three good, but lesser, men died trying.† In addition,
Ballinger had heard the wildest stories about Dusty
Fog's speed and accuracy when using a matched brace
of Army Colts; stories the detective knew could not
possibly be true. He found himself looking forward to
meeting this giant among men and seeing how close
Texas' favorite son came to his reputation.

While making the fire, Ballinger had removed his hat,
jacket, collar and tie. The night proved to be warm
enough for him to leave them off and doing so probably
saved his life.

Suddenly a shape loomed up from the darkness; a
man wearing range clothes, a deputy's badge, and
carrying a revolver. Without saying a word, the
newcomer started to swing his weapon towards the
detective. Ballinger reacted fast, flinging himself backwards in a desperate attempt to reach his jacket and
draw the Smith and Wesson from its pocket. Even as he
moved, the detective saw Red take evasive action in a
similar manner, by throwing himself over and away
from the fire's light. Then Red passed out of Ballinger's
sight, the detective being more concerned with watching
the man with the gun trying to correct his aim. A shot
roared, but not from the newcomer's weapon. Struck by
a bullet, Ballinger figured it must have been fired by
Red, the deputy jerked on to his toes. The revolver
barked and its bullet ploughed into the ground some
distance from where Ballinger landed.

Red landed on his side, thumb-cocking the Colt on its
recoil and ready to shoot again. Too late he saw the
second shape. More prudent, this one, and better
armed; he stayed back in the half light at the edge of the
fire's glow, a rifle in his hands. Like his companion, the

---

* Told in *The Ysabel Kid.*
† Told in *Quiet Town.*

man seemed set on shooting Ballinger. However he recognized Red as the more serious threat and changed his aim. Red knew he could not turn his gun, aim and fire in time to save himself.

Flame lanced in the blackness on the opposite side of the camp to the attackers and the flat bark of a Winchester split the night. The second man suddenly jerked, his own rifle spitting and sending a bullet over Red's body, spun around and crashed to the ground.

"That's all of them, Red," called a voice from the direction of the life-saving rifle. "Don't you go shooting me in the leg as I come out."

"Come ahead, you damned Comanche," Red answered, rising to his feet and watching the two still shapes. "Are you all right, Ed?"

"He missed me," Ballinger answered. "Th—"

The words died off as a tall young man materialized in the firelight. The all black clothing, hat, bandana, short levis down to boots, tended to merge with the surrounding darkness. Black hair showed from under the low crowned, Texas-style hat. Ballinger glanced at the Winchester '66 rifle in the other's hands, then lifted his eyes to the face. Tanned, almost Indian dark, the features looked handsome and almost babyishly innocent – except for the wild, red-hazel eyes. Such old, experienced eyes did not go with so young and innocent a face. In addition to the rifle, the newcomer wore a gunbelt with a walnut handled Dragoon Colt butt forward at his right side and an ivory hilted James Black bowie knife sheathed at the left.

Moving forward with a silent, long-stepping stride, the young man held his rifle ready for use and did not relax until he had reached the second attacker, kicked aside the fallen weapon and made sure that no danger threatened. Red repeated the process with the man he shot. Watching the Texans, Ballinger could not help being struck by the smoothly efficient manner in which they worked.

"They're lawmen," the detective said, joining Red and looking down at the body.

"Jack City lawmen," Red corrected. "And better stock than those three who jumped us this afternoon."

"Could be the same," Ballinger objected.

"This one's a good gun. He wouldn't've missed when he shot at us," Red answered. "Seemed mighty eager to get *you*, both of them."

"Looked mighty set on doing it too," the dark youngster remarked, strolling back. "Hondo told us where you'd gone, Red, and Dusty told me'n' the boy to come over in case you found trouble. When we saw the fire here, I figured I'd come in on foot and see who it was. Heard them two crashing about just after I got here, but it was too late to yell."

"I'm not sorry you happened along, Lon," Red admitted, ignoring the sound of approaching horses. "This here's Ed – Farrel, he's a travelling salesman. Ed, meet Loncey Dalton Ysabel. You've maybe heard more of him as the Ysabel Kid?"

"Pleased to know you, friend, and grateful," Ballinger said, holding out his hand.

"Howdy," answered the Ysabel Kid, shaking hands but eyeing Ballinger critically and with just a hint of suspicion.

Although Ballinger did not realize it, he was looking at a living legend. Down on the Rio Grande nobody would have needed telling that Loncey Dalton Ysabel mostly went under the name of the Ysabel Kid. From his early days, with a brief interlude riding scout in the Grey Ghost, John Singleton Mosby's Raiders, the Kid rode the border river as a smuggler. He spoke fluent Spanish and Comanche probably better than English, it being his mother tongue. His father was a wild Irish-Kentuckian, his mother the daughter of Chief Long Walker and his French Creole squaw. In his childhood, the Kid went through the initiation of the Comanche

Dog Soldiers Lodge and still had access to its élite ranks. From his instructors among the cream of the horse-Indians, he learned to ride anything with hair, follow a trail by the smallest of signs, use eyes, ears and nose when on a scouting mission and other useful things. He was good, but not exceptional, with his Dragoon Colt; a skilled performer when handling his bowie knife; but an absolute maestro in the use of the brass-framed Winchester known fondly as the "old yellow boy."

One way and another, it paid to have a dangerous young man like the Ysabel Kid as a friend. He did not seem to like Ballinger.

Four horses came out of the darkness, although only one of them carried a rider. A magnificent white stallion led the way, stepping proudly and looking as wild and mean as a bull elk bugling out a challenge in spring, and leading a second horse which was tied to its saddle. Seated on a large paint stallion and leading a good sorrel, a tall cowhand even younger than Red or the Kid approached the others. Every inch of his clothing spelled Texas cowhand – and a good one to eyes which knew the West. He had curly blond hair, a tanned, intelligent and handsome young face which might smile easily under the right conditions. Around his waist hung a gunbelt and even his youth did nothing to relieve the impression of competence with which he carried the matched staghorn butted Army Colts in their open-topped holsters.

"Hi, Red," greeted the youngster, speaking in a friendly Texas drawl like both the others. "Ole Dusty's sure riled about you coming here all alone. He's going to fix your wagon good when he sees you."

"Somebody had to do something, boy," Red replied. "And you bunch were still fooling around with the gals in Mulrooney."

"We sure was," agreed the youngster, grinning as he

thought of the hectic days spent running the law in the newly-opened Kansas trail-end town of Mulrooney.*

On being introduced to the second newcomer – who appeared to have only one name, Waco – Ballinger again became aware of a slightly critical scrutiny and wondered at it. He also wondered what kind of youngster the other might be.

Waco was a product of his age. Left an orphan almost from birth by a Waco Indian raid, he had been raised as part of a large ranch family. At thirteen he left home, riding out to seek adventure. Even then he wore a gun and knew how to use it. By sixteen he was well on the trail which turned Wes Hardin, Bill Longley and many another Texas boy on to the wanted list. Riding as a member of Clay Allison's wild onion crew was not the way back to a respectable, useful life. While on a trail drive with Allison's C.A., Waco met Dusty Fog when the other saved him from death under a stampede.† From that day on Waco started to change for the better. He joined Dusty and made the other his model, losing all his truculent, suspicious ways, learning much from his new friends and fast developing into a useful member of rangeland society.

"Who are they, Red?" asked Waco, nodding to the two bodies.

"A couple of Jack City guns," Red answered.

"What're we going to do with them?" Ballinger inquired, wondering how he, a duly appointed peace officer, should act in the matter.

"Send them back to Jack City," replied the Kid.

"Take them back?" Ballinger said.

"Nope, Mr. Farrel," the Kid drawled. "*Send* them back. Their hosses are out that ways a piece, boy. Go bring 'em in."

---

* Told in *The Trouble Busters*.
† Told in *Trigger Fast*.

"How come I get all the work to do?" demanded Waco, but he went to obey without waiting for an answer.

Watching Waco depart, Red marvelled at the change wrought in only a few short months.

"He's a damned good kid," the Kid remarked.

"Sure is," agreed Red, and turned to Ballinger. "Only, was I you, Ed, I'd not call him 'boy' until you know him better."

"Man'd say those Jack City boys wanted to kill you a bit, mister," the Kid said, also giving Ballinger his attention.

"Were riled about the fight we started in the saloon maybe," Ballinger replied, unaware that if a Texan called one "mister" after being introduced, he did not care for the person he addressed.

"Could be," Red went on. "Or maybe they don't like the kind of soap you sell, Ed. Looked like they aimed to drop you first. Say, did that jasper you threw the bottle at know you from some place?"

"He could have," admitted Ballinger cautiously. "I've been around."

Red eyed Ballinger for a long moment before giving a shrug and turning his attention to where hooves sounded from the direction in which Waco had disappeared. In a few minutes the youngster returned, leading a couple of horses. Ignoring Ballinger, the three Texans loaded one body across each saddle and secured them in position. Ballinger stood watching and trying to decide if he should insist on more formal treatment of the bodies, but before he reached any decision, the horses had been pointed in the direction of Jack City, released, slapped on the rump and sent off into the darkness carrying their grisly burdens.

"Are you sure it'll be all right?" he asked, with visions of two horses roaming the Texas ranges carrying corpses across their saddles.

"A range hoss'll always go home, given its head," the Kid answered. "And I'm for sure not getting on the blister end of a shovel to bury any cheap hired gun."

"That's for certain sure," agreed Waco. "What now, Lon?"

"Best thing'd be to get away from here," the Kid replied. "There might be more of 'em looking for Red and Mr. Farrel. And if not, there'll likely be when the bodies get back to Jack City. Which same, the lake here's the first place they'll look. We'll push on for home."

"The bay's lame, Lon," Red pointed out.

"And our horses are tuckered out," Waco continued.

"Looks that way," agreed the Kid. "Reckon you'd better take that sorrel, Mr. Farrel. We'll push on for a couple of miles and make a dry camp clear of the trail."

"Be best," Red agreed. "Even if Jack City send out a posse, they can't read sign in the dark. I don't reckon they'll chance following us too close to Rio Hondo County comes morning either."

CHAPTER ELEVEN

Lieutenant Ballinger Learns
Something

Red Blaze proved to be a shrewd prophet. Shortly after noon the following day, the detective and three Texans rode along the main street of Polveroso, seat of Rio Hondo County. Slightly bigger, cleaner and better set out than Jack City, Polveroso still looked like a hamlet to Ballinger's big-city eyes. What struck him was the number of business premises which bore the names Hardin, Blaze or Fog over their doors. It came almost as a shock to see "Smith's Hardware Store" on the building.

"We're trying to move him on," Red remarked, making the invariable joke of the Polveroso citizen when a stranger commented on the non-clan name.

"He's the only cuss in town worth knowing," the Kid went on.

After leaving their horses in the civic pound, the Texans led Ballinger to the stone building which housed the local law enforcement offices and jail. Entering the office of the marshal and county sheriff – both positions being held by the same man – Ballinger was impressed by the clean, tidy orderliness of the big room. Wanted posters and other notices hung on a board by the right of the main door, a hatrack at the left. On one wall, in a rack, stood three Winchesters, four twin-barrelled ten-gauge shotguns and a Sharps Old Reliable buffalo rifle. A safe, several chairs and a desk completed the furnishings. The desk's top had only a few papers on it, and an open book which Ballinger took to be the blotter, although he never expected to see one until returning to civilization.

From the first, Ballinger liked what he saw of Sheriff Hondo Fog. A tall, tanned man wearing clean, neat range clothes and belting a low hanging Army Colt, the sheriff gave an impression of competence and capability. "Got that bottle from the Tumbleweed, Uncle Hondo," Red announced.

"Take it down to your Uncle Barnes' office when you go," Hondo answered. "Did you run into any trouble getting it?"

"Had a mite."

"Get into a fight?" asked Hondo, knowing his nephew's way of attracting trouble and becoming involved in fights.

"Had one forced on me," Red corrected.

"And I bet you backed off a mile to avoid it," grinned the sheriff, throwing a meaning glance at Ballinger.

"This's Ed Farrel," Red introduced. "Sided me in the saloon. He's a soap salesman, but I've never seen such a Jim-Dandy way of fighting. Got hold of a brush handle and sure made it talk. He handled five-six men with it and they never had a chance."

With numberous gestures, Red went on to describe how Ballinger used the brush handle while Hondo watched with interest. At last the sheriff turned his attention to Ballinger.

"How about showing me your badge, Mr. – Farrel?"

"Badge?" countered Ballinger, almost instinctively.

A slight frown came to Hondo's face. "Are you a Pinkerton man?" he growled, for members of the Pinkerton Detective Agency were not popular in the Southern States.

"Like hell I am a pink eye!" Ballinger snorted, before he could stop himself.

"Which means you're official law," Hondo stated, with a smile. "Wouldn't've got that riled at being taken for a Pinkerton otherwise."

If Ballinger had needed more confirmation, the words gave it. There stood a mighty shrewd country lawman; quick enough to know what the skill at fighting shown by Ballinger meant. Taking out his identification wallet, he passed it to the sheriff.

"The name's Ballinger—"

"We don't go much on saying 'mister' in Texas," Hondo interrupted.

"Ed Ballinger. I'm a detective-lieutenant out of Chicago."

"Knew all along you were law of some kind," Red commented.

"Figured the way you hid it, you must be a Pinkerton snoop," the Kid went on, losing his unfriendliness.

"Button it up, both of you," Hondo ordered. "Don't you have any work to do at the spread?"

"Not if we can avoid Dusty," Waco grinned.

"In any case, he's coming down this ways," Hondo warned, and turned back to Ballinger. "Mind if they stay on and hear what you've got to say? Shows you what I have to suffer. These are my deputies."

"His *unpaid* deputies," the Kid corrected.

"I offered to pay you what you're worth," Hondo pointed out. "But you reckoned you couldn't work for nothing."

Listening and watching, Ballinger knew that behind the banter lay a mutual respect and trust. Before he could speak, the front door opened and two men entered the office.

From what Ballinger had heard, he knew one of the newcomers to be the famous Dusty Fog. Studying the golden blond hair, almost classically handsome face, six-foot-three of height, great spread of shoulders, slim

waist and enormous muscular development of the taller
man, Ballinger reckoned that he might be capable of
performing most of the deeds attributed to Dusty Fog.
Something of a dandy dresser, his clothing expensive
and made to fit his giant frame, he was still a man's man
and the ivory handled Army Colts in the holsters of his
gunbelt looked to be functional rather than decorative
weapons.

Compared with the blond giant, the second man
rarely rated a second glance, despite the fact that he
carried a brace of bone handled Army Colts butt forward in opened topped holsters. Or did he? Although
not more than five-foot-six tall, he possessed a powerful
frame – one which would have equalled his companion's
had they both been the same height. Dressed in good
quality clothing, he did not show them to their best advantage. He had dusty blond hair and a strong, intelligent, handsome face. Studying the second man
more carefully, Ballinger found that the other had the
build of a pocket Hercules and gained an impression of
strength of character that went beyond mere feet and
inches.

"See you're back," said the small man, eyeing Red
up and down.

"Just now got in, Cousin Dusty," Red replied.

With something like a shock, Ballinger realized that
he had guessed wrong. The small man was Dusty Fog. A
moment later the detective found himself being formally
introduced to the fabulous Texan and the blond giant,
Mark Counter.

While Ballinger did not know it right then, Mark
Counter bore quite a name himself. It was claimed that
Mark's skill with cattle exceeded Dusty Fog's. His
strength had become legendary and his prowess in a
rough-house brawl something never forgotten. The son
of one of the richest men in Texas, and wealthy in his
own right, Mark elected to ride as a hand at the O.D.
Connected—not an ordinary hand, but a member of the

élite of the crew, Ole Devil's floating outfit. In addition to his other skills, folks who *knew* claimed Mark to be second only to Dusty Fog in the matter of handling a matched brace of Army Colts.

"Suppose we start it off, paw?" suggested Dusty, as they took seats around the desk. "Tell Ed what we know."

"Sure," agreed Hondo. "Starting about six months ago, Ed, we began to hear stories about Jack City. It was growing, getting a reputation for being a real wide open town. The kind of place that draws cowhands like steel to a magnet. Most of the hands who went came back broke. Some came back bad hurt. A few never came back at all. Jack City's over the county line and I couldn't do a thing beyond warning off the local hands."

"Do you know who's behind the sudden growth?" Ballinger asked.

"An Eastern jasper called Harte owns the Tumbleweed and a place outside town," Hondo answered. "Last week a representative of Dennison's Old Whipping Post came to see me and claimed that sales of his whisky were dropping all over Texas and New Mexico. Yet saloons had their shelves loaded with full bottles and it kept selling. Which meant moonshining."

"You mean illegally distilling whisky?"

"Sure. There're a lot of Kentuckian hill-folks in John County and it's always been a hot-bed of moonshining. Hasn't it, Lon?"

"So they do tell me," answered the Kid evasively.

"Anyway, I don't know if you know it, Ed, but there're tests which can tell just which distillery made a particular brand of whisky. We figured to pick up a bottle in Jack City and compare it with some old stock bought from a John County still-runner. That's what took Red to Jack City."

"There's more than just moonshining though, paw," Dusty guessed.

"A whole heap more," Hondo agreed. "There's a whole lot more smuggling than ever since Sam Ysabel finished. Only it's not the sort Sam and Lon did. They traded locally. The new bunch cover a whole lot of the Southern States and they're costing the Government hundreds of thousand dollars in lost revenue. Likely it's all being handled through Jack City. At least there's a big freight business being run out of there."

"Can't the law do anything?" Ballinger asked.

"John County's got about as much law as an egg has milk," Hondo replied. "The Texas Rangers can't move in without being called by the local authorities and a couple of U.S. Secret Service men who arrived disappeared almost as quick."

"This Harte came from the East you say, paw," Dusty put in. "Ed's from Chicago. There couldn't be anything in it, could there?"

"You might say there is," Ballinger smiled, then started to tell the full story of why he came to Texas. He covered everything that might help his task, including the incident at the Tumbleweed and the attempted murder on the range.

"Looks like that Lighthouse jasper sent men out to finish you, Ed," Dusty stated. "If you'd been wearing those dude hat, jacket and tie, they'd have been sure it was you and not moved in. How'd you figured to take this Reckharts and Lash when you reached Texas?"

"I hadn't made any plans, but figured to get some help from the local law."

"They do say Jason Lash's fair with a gun," Waco remarked. "How well can you shoot, Ed?"

"I sometimes hit what I'm aiming at," Ballinger answered.

"Man has to have a gun to hit anything," the Kid commented dryly.

"I've a gun all right."

Taking out his much prized Smith and Wesson revolver, Ed Ballinger showed it to the Texans. The result was not what he expected.

"You call *that* a gun?" asked the Kid.

"If you aim to tangle with Reckhart's men," warned Dusty, "you'd best get something better than an itty-bitty stingy gun – or make your will."

Looking at the .32 calibre revolver, Mark nodded. "Was I a praying man, I'd say 'Amen' to that."

"Sure is the fiercest gun I ever saw," drawled Waco.

"I can hit what I aim at with it," Ballinger protested.

"Which is fine, as long as it's not something that can shoot back," the Kid stated.

"Hold hard there!" Hondo barked. "Things stand this way, Ed. If we can get evidence against Harte, or Reckharts, then I'm willing to say to hell with the county line and move. Also the Rangers can take a hand without a call from John County's law. But we must have evidence. Gathering it'll take time. How about it, Lon, can you talk to the moonshiners?"

"And put them behind bars?" growled the Kid.

"We never jailed one yet. But that was while they did it on a small scale. Now it's big and growing bigger."

"Which's what I don't get," the Kid said. "I know those folks. They make a mountain-dew, but not enough for it to be hard work. Getting out as much as you say they're doing would make too much sweat for them to do it."

"Only they're doing it," Dusty pointed out.

"That's what I don't like," the Kid answered. "I'll take – damn it, I can't go. There's that business up at grandpappy's reservation needs handling."

"Sure. And you'll have to pull out tomorrow for it," Dusty agreed. "With those jaspers from Washington attending, you can't miss it."

"I forgot about that," Hondo admitted. "There's some trouble on the Comanche reservation. Lon's grandfather doesn't take to talking direct and can't trust the usual run of interpreters. So Lon's going up to speak for him. Won't be back for two-three weeks."

"Can't we make a start without him?" asked Ballinger.

"Sure, and get nowhere," Hondo replied. "Those hill-folks are mighty close-mouthed except to somebody they know and trust."

"The time'll give us a chance to get ready," Dusty went on. "You figure to take Lash yourself, Ed?"

It was a statement rather than a question. No lawman worth the name took lead and had a fellow officer shot down by his side without making every effort to bring in the man who did it.

"I aim to get him," Ballinger agreed.

"How'd he pull his gun when he came through the door that day?" asked Dusty.

"He didn't. Had it in his hand and shot from waist high. He must have been real lucky to hit me like that. He was easy thirty foot away."

Hondo and Dusty exchanged glances. Then the sheriff looked at the others. "Red, take that Tumbleweed whisky to the judge's office," he ordered.

"Mark," Dusty continued, "head for the ranch. Take the boy with you. If Joe Gaylin's there, ask him to wait until I come out. If he's left, send Waco after him. I want him to come back. Tell him it's *real* important, boy."

"Yo!" answered Waco, giving the old cavalry response.

"Tell Uncle Devil that I'll be out later, Mark," Dusty finished. "And go out to make sure that the crew're tending to that shipping bunch."

"Huh!" grunted Waco, eyeing the Kid in disgust. "See our Injun brother's having an easy life."

"Don't he always," answered Mark. "Let's go, boy."

After the departure of the three young men, Hondo turned his attention to Ballinger. "How about taking a stroll with us, Ed?"

"Be pleased to," Ballinger replied, knowing that the

other was not merely passing the time of day.

Accompanied by Dusty and the Kid, Ballinger followed Hondo from the office. During the walk through the back streets of the town, the detective mentioned his deserted bag at Jack City.

"Is there anything important in it?" Dusty asked.

"Only clothes, and a few soap samples," Ballinger answered. "I had all the documents in my grip."

"Then we'll leave it a piece. I don't want to lead them to you. Sure they'll be looking for you, but leave us not make it any easier for them."

Before Dusty could enlarge on his statement, they left the town behind them and entered a blind draw. At one end stood a rail with a number of bottles on it and to its left a target made out of sheet iron worked into the shape of a full-sized, standing man. Numerous indentations on the target showed that it had often been used – and hit.

Halting some thirty foot from the target, Hondo indicated it. "Let's see you hit that, Ed."

"Whereabouts?" smiled Ballinger.

"About where his heart would be."

Ballinger took his revolver out, turned sideways to the target and assumed a classic shooting posture. In his desire to make a good showing, he took his time in taking aim. If so short a distance was the best at which a Western man could hit his mark, Ballinger figured he could handle Lash without help. Three times the Smith and Wesson spat, its bullets making faint clangs as they struck the target in a neat, small triangle on the heart area. Lowering the gun, he turned to the watching Texans but could read nothing from their faces.

"Lon," Hondo said.

Stepping to where Ballinger had stood, the Kid halted. His right hand turned palm out, closed on the walnut handle of the heavy old Dragoon and brought it out of the holster. Coming across, his left hand locked and gave support to the right and held the gun in the centre of his body, waist high. Almost instantly, with a deep, coughing bellow, the Dragoon fired. Only this time the target vibrated and clanged viciously when the lead stuck it in what would have been a human being's navel.

"Not the heart," said the Kid, blowing smoke from the Dragoon's barrel, "but I don't figure he'd've argued about it."

"Great day in the morning!" Ballinger gasped. "I've never seen anything so fast."

"*Fast?*" yelped the Kid. "Land-sakes, Ed, I'm not fast at all."

"But you – " the detective began, not noticing that Dusty had moved into position on the line.

"Dusty!" Hondo said.

Almost before Ballinger had turned his eyes towards the firing line, Dusty handed him the shock of his life. On the word from his father, Dusty's hands crossed so fast the eye could barely follow their movements. Steel rasped on leather as the guns left their holsters to roar in the small Texan's hands. Once again the target rang to the impact of lead, although Ballinger could not differentiate between the sounds of the two shots. He just stood staring at Dusty in open-mouthed amazement; yet he might have been more impressed had he examined the target – the two bullets struck home almost on the impact area of the detective's three shots. There was one small thing to remember. From deciding to shoot to getting off his first bullet took Ballinger almost two seconds. Dusty drew, shot and hit the same mark in just over an eighth of that time.

"I saw it, but I don't believe it!" Ballinger gasped.

"You'd have a hard time telling that target it didn't happen," drawled the Kid. "Either way, you'd best learn how to handle your gun a mite faster happen you aim to go after Lash. He might not be one of the top guns, but he's a whole heap too fast for you to take that much time when you meet him."

"Lon's right, Ed," Hondo confirmed.

"You want to get a real gun, too," the Kid went on.

"This's a real gun!" Ballinger objected.

"Shoots mighty straight too," admitted the Kid. "Only not when you're a lawman and have to wait for him to make the first move. Even a Navy Colt's not big enough then, and it shoots a .36 ball."

"Lon's right, Ed," Hondo warned. "This's not Chicago. You're in Texas now. Every man, damned near every boy over thirteen, totes a gun and knows how to use it. When you go after Lash and Reckharts, you'll need to be ready to shoot. Sure, I know you can shoot accurately – with that light gun – but you'd be dead before you got it out."

"And even if you got it out and hit the other feller," said the Kid, "unless you smacked him right between his two eyes, he'd still be able to stand and shoot back."

So deadly serious did the two men sound and accompany the statements by mutual confirmatory nods, that Ballinger felt convinced. Already he had seen that they knew what they talked about. He must discard his preconceived ideas and take all the help he could obtain.

"What'd be best for me to do?" he asked.

"I'd say learn to handle a gun our way," Hondo answered. "Stay on here to do it. We'll put feelers out, gather any odd scraps of information we can until Lon gets back. Then we'll start bearing down on John County to see what pops."

"I'll help you all I can," Dusty promised. "Only we'll take you out to the ranch. Most likely Reckharts'll send men after you, knowing why you're here. If there's going to be fuss it can be easiest handled away from town."

"Whatever you say," Ballinger replied. "I'm putting myself in your hands."

CHAPTER TWELVE

Lieutenant Ballinger Acquires a
New Skill

"First though," Dusty said, "I don't reckon your boss'd want you walking the rounds wearing a buscadero gunbelt like mine."

"It wouldn't go down very well," Ballinger admitted with a grin.

"So what we need is a gun that's small enough to be carried hidden under your jacket, but that packs a good, heavy bullet."

"A Remington Double Derringer?" suggested the detective. "They come at .41."

"And only carry two bullets. You may go your whole life without needing even the second shot. But if you need more than two, there's no time to start trying to reload."

"Hey now," Hondo put in. "Go down to the hardware store, Dusty. Ask Jubal to show you that gun he had shipped in from the East. I'll go see about that whisky."

"Reckon I'd best head for the ranch and get ready to pull out," the Kid went on. "See you when I get back, Ed."

The party separated about its individual businesses. Dusty and Ballinger returned to town and made their way to the hardware store. Inside Ballinger found a good selection of arms, ammunition, powder, percussion caps, lead for making bullets and everything else a shooting man might require. At Dusty's request, the owner – who proved to be an uncle by marriage – produced a short barrelled, heavy looking revolver.

"A Webley Bulldog," he said. ".41 in calibre, six shots, takes a rimfire metal cartridge."

Taking the gun, Dusty hefted it, whirled it on his trigger finger and tested its balance.

"Can't say I like it, but I've been using my old Army Colts for too long to make a change."

Dusty did eventually make a change in weapons, but not until the Colt company bought out the finest *fighting* revolver of them all, the famous Model P in 1873.*

"Feels all right to me," Ballinger commented, accepting the gun.

"Can we buy it, Uncle Jubal?"

"I had bought it for keeping under the counter," Smith answered. "But if you're set on having it—"

"It could mean the difference between life and death for Ed," Dusty said.

"Take it then. I'll stick to my sawed-off until I can get another shipped out. There's two hundred and fifty bullets and a reloading outfit go with it."

"I'll take it," Ballinger decided. "Sure hope I can get some of the price back from the city as expense money."

"There'll be a mite more to pay for yet," Dusty warned. "You can't carry a gun in your pocket and draw it fast. We're going to need a holster for you, but what kind, I don't know."

At that time no big city law enforcement organization troubled much over arming its officers. Consequently nobody knew much about how a detective should carry his handgun. Ballinger had not the faintest idea of what might be needed. However two things stood in his

* Told in *The Peacemakers*.

favor: the firearm's savvy of the Rio Hondo gun wizard, Dusty Fog, and the knowledge and skill of one of the finest holster makers and general leather workers in the West.

On arrival at the headquarters of the great O.D. Connected ranch, Ballinger was introduced to its owner, Ole Devil Hardin, and a short, gnarled old man with skin like the leather he worked so well. Joe Gaylin, on one of his periodic visits, listened to Ballinger's problem and sat for a time without speaking; but in that time his eyes never left the detective's waist region. At last Gaylin grunted a request to see the gun. Taking out the Webley, Ballinger handed it over and watched as Gaylin examined it. Rising, the old man held the gun against his hip, shook his head and lifted it higher.

"Pointing the butt to the rear won't work," he stated. "It'd be too high to be drawn."

"How about putting it at the left, drawing cross-hand?" asked Dusty.

Again Gaylin held the gun in position, moving it around. "You wear a waistbelt, young feller?" he inquired.

"Sure," Ballinger answered.

"It'll need to be a mite wider than that'n," Gaylin said, as Ballinger exposed the belt. "I can fix that easy enough. Get me a sheet of paper, Dusty. I reckon I can fix what we need."

On receiving the paper, Gaylin took the stub of a pencil from his pocket and sketched out a pattern. He handed the Webley back to Ballinger and stated that he worked best without a swarm of folks looking over his shoulder.

"We'll go out back and see how the gun shoots, Ed," Dusty suggested.

Some distance behind the big house was an area somewhat similar to the one in which Ballinger learned his first lesson in the art of Western gun handling. Instead of using the man-shaped target, he was requested to try his aim upon one of more formal pattern and by taking sight rather than attempting to fire in instinctive alignment. After letting off one shot, Ballinger knew why Dusty made the suggestion. The short-barrelled Webley roared loud, kicked hard, and took more handling than his Smith and Wesson.

"I didn't know I was this bad," Ballinger told Dusty ruefully as he examined the target.

"You're just not used to the gun," Dusty replied. "I'll have Uncle Jubal come out and work on its innards: lighten the trigger-pull and generally smooth it over. That'll ease it for you, but you'll have to learn to live with its kick."

"Do you want me to shoot some more?"

"No point in wasting bullets, even if we do intend to reload them. Let's go back to the house."

"Reckon I'll shave this lot off," Ballinger remarked, as they returned, indicating his beard. "Reckharts knows I'm around now, so there's no point in keeping it on."

At the house, they found that Jubal Smith had anticipated the need for his services and come out from town bringing his tools ready to work on the Webley's mechanism.

Ballinger found that everybody in the big house willingly assisted him. First Ole Devil, tied to a wheelchair since failing to ride the big paint stallion Dusty used as his personal mount,* gave him the freedom of the building. Then each member of the floating outfit prepared to weigh in with his considerable experience in matters of gun-handling. Even the black-haired, petite and beautiful Betty Hardin, Ole Devil's granddaughter, joined in the conference which took place after supper that evening.

Leaving the dining room, Ole Devil, Betty, the floating outfit and Ballinger – the latter now clad in an

___
* Told in *The Fastest Gun in Texas*.

open-necked shirt and levis pants – gathered in the big
study. Ballinger looked at the shelves, loaded with well-
read books, that flanked one wall; then turned his eyes
to the collection of handguns and rifles decorating the
others. Never had he seen such a variety of weapons and
he hoped to be able to examine them at his leisure.

"That Webley shoots double-action, doesn't it?"
Waco asked, sitting between Mark and Betty.

"Sure," agreed Dusty. "Which means that Ed
doesn't have to thumb-cock it before he can shoot,
although it's quicker to do so."

"Wouldn't say that," the youngster objected. "There
was a feller rode with Clay Allison. He used a Starr
Army and always worked it double-action. Had it timed
so that he started squeezing the trigger as soon as he
took hold and the hammer fell as soon as the gun
lined."

"Now there's a thought," Dusty replied. "Go get me
that Starr off the wall, boy."

"Wish I hadn't thought of the blamed idea now,"
grunted Waco, but rose and collected a Starr Army
revolver from its place on the wall.

Taking the gun, Dusty checked that it was unloaded –
although he knew it must be, he did not fail to take the
basic precaution – and thrust it into his waistband at the
left side. Without any attempt at speed, his right hand
crossed, gripped the Starr's butt, forefinger entering the
trigger guard and starting to squeeze. Long before the
gun came clear and into line; a dry click announced that
the hammer had risen and fallen.

"You'd've made a hole in your ribs then," Mark
commented.

On his second attempt, Dusty managed to have the
gun pointing away from him but not satisfactorily.

"You'd've blown a hole in my foot that time," Mark
guessed.

"Good thing too," Waco put in, and ducked as a big
hand swung in the direction of his head.

"If you pair want to horse around, try the corral," Betty warned. "I don't want this room mussing up."

"Dang women shouldn't be in here anyway," Mark answered, then raised his hands as Betty came to her feet. "No offence, ma'am. It was all Waco's fault."

Nor was the surrender an entire fake. Like Dusty, Betty had learned ju-jitsu and karate from her grandfather's Japanese servant. She could handle even a man as strong as Mark given the chance of obtaining one of the painful holds.

"It mostly is," she commented.

Despite the levity Ballinger learned much about practical gun-handling. He remarked that an instructor in the Provost Marshal's Department taught that one should get off a shot as quickly as possible, even if it did no more than kick up a spurt of dirt into the target's face and distract him.

"Could be," admitted Dusty. "Happen you're so fast you can chance giving the other man that much of an edge. Me, I've always found that putting lead *into* the man puts him off a damned sight more certain than trying to blind him by kicking dirt into his face."

"There's some who might mention the sanctity of human life," Ballinger said.

"Sure," agreed Dusty. "But I never yet asked any man to try to kill me; and I figure my life's worth as much to me as his is to him. Just the same, if he throws down on me, I reckon it's my right to stop him – even if I have to kill him to do it."

"After what happened to Donovan, I reckon I agree with you," Ballinger replied. "Let's see if I can get this squeezing business worked out."

Before he could attempt the tricky piece of gun handling, Ballinger saw Gaylin enter the room carrying a roughly made holster.

"Just want to get the set of it right afore I do any more," the old leather-worker said. "Got your gun, friend?"

"There's a Webley Bulldog on the wall," Betty remarked. "It's a .45, but not much different in size to your gun, Ed."

"I know, I know," groaned Waco, coming to his feet. "Go get it, boy. One of these days—"

Leaving the threat hanging in the air, the youngster crossed to the wall and took down a worn old Webley Bulldog. With the weapon in the holster, Ballinger was told to try her for fit. Attaching the loop of the holster to his belt, Ballinger moved it back and forwards until he found the most comfortable position. To Western eyes, the holster appeared to ride high and slightly far forward, but it felt comfortable and would be concealed by the jacket. To make sure of that point, Waco found himself sent to Ballinger's room and returned carrying the detective's coat. Once dressed, Ballinger stood up and received the Texans' verdict that no better concealment could be obtained in a position where the gun would be easily accessible to the right hand and comfortable.

"Once you start wearing it, Ed," Dusty said, explaining the point, "get into the habit of strapping it on in the morning and wearing it all day. More than one peace officer's died because he took his gun off in the office and didn't have time to put it back on again when somebody came after him. So make sure the holster fits comfortable, then you won't be tempted to take it off."

After the incident at Reckharts' mansion, Ballinger knew that Dusty spoke the truth and did not intend to be caught out in the same manner again.

When the holster had been set right, Gaylin took it away to change its rough lines into the finest product of the holster-maker's art available. Ballinger spent the rest of the evening practicing the trigger-squeeze and found that he soon mastered its control to a certain extent. The difficulty would come later.

Next morning found Ballinger on the shooting range behind the house and handling his Webley. Smith had worked all night to smooth out the gun's operation and the results showed quickly. During the evening Dusty reloaded several bullets with a light powder charge, and using these Ballinger gained the feel of the gun. However the small Texan insisted that Ballinger waited until he could shoot *aimed* scores, using a full charged round, as good as with the Smith and Wesson before allowing him to try working by instinctive alignment. By late afternoon he found himself able to line the gun, take sight and send shot after shot into the centre of the target. The way lay clear for him to learn the most difficult part of the business, as soon as he was given his holster.

The last proved to take longer than Ballinger anticipated. Shortly before nightfall, Gaylin produced a well-made holster. Small, compact, leaving clear the gun's trigger guard and butt, the holster showed signs of the thought and care which went into its production. However Ballinger found that he could not just place his Webley home and start practising.

"I allus make a holster just a shade too small for a start," Gaylin explained. "See, Ed, while you can stretch it a mite, there's no way you can shrink well-tanned leather. We'll dump her in the hoss trough to soak, and don't worry, it won't hurt the leather. While I'm doing that, you'd best oil that Webley inside and out so I can block the holster when it's soaked."

After a couple of hours' soaking in the horse trough, the holster was removed. Gaylin shook off the excess moisture and brought the holster into the study. Inserting the oiled revolver, he checked to make sure that it sat squarely before kneading the now-supple leather to the contours of the gun. When satisfied, Gaylin set the holster, still holding the Webley, aside to dry all night.

If Ballinger hoped to make a start the following morning, he was disappointed. Although he received his gun, the holster needed at least two days to dry out completely. However his time was not wasted. Much powder burned and lead passed through the Webley's stubby barrel as he worked to improve his aim. In addition he spent hours in trying to perfect the trigger squeeze. Starting with the gun in his waistband, empty cartridge cases in the chambers to protect the hammer, he repeatedly sent his hand across to the butt, closed his fingers, inserting the first into the trigger guard and trying to time the squeeze so that the click came as the barrel lined on the target.

During the late afternoon of the second day, Dusty decided that Ballinger had improved enough to use live bullets. Not that the detective drew fast, but he appeared to have mastered trigger control. Then another snag appeared. While Ballinger looked likely to shoot himself, or spray off lead wildly to one side, he found swinging the gun across made instinctive alignment far harder than when just raising the gun into position. Time after time he completed a good move, ending with his elbow central to his belt buckle, forearm parallel to the ground, whole body aimed straight at the target; only to see dirt spurt up on one side or the other of it and indicate another miss. Even receiving the holster and working from it did not help with the problem of halting the aim.

Dusty knew instinctively what caused the difficulty. While the seven and a half inch barrel of the Army Colt lent itself to that style of shooting, the two inches of the Webley's snout did not. One could just about see the nose of an Army lining, but not the shorter Webley and a slight error at the shooting end meant a clean miss on a target the width of an average human body.

It was a time of annoyance and frustration for Ballinger. Three days went by without his making any improvement in his aim. Dusty sensed how the detective must feel, knowing younger men could perform the feat he tried so hard to learn. So when he saw signs that Ballinger felt like quitting, he called a halt and steered the conversation on to the modern developments in criminal investigation, or persuaded the detective to teach him the art of baton-fighting. Doing this gave Ballinger's ego a badly-needed boost by allowing him to display some superior knowledge, and smoothed over his feeling of incompetence.

Mark and Waco saw little of Ballinger during the first week, being out on the far ranges of the ranch. On Tuesday of the second week, they returned to the house and gathered in the study after dinner. As usual Mark settled down in his favorite easy chair and listened to the talk. Studying the gun, which Ballinger wore all day even in the house so as to become accustomed to feeling it on him, a thought struck the blond giant.

"Hey, Ed," he said, "how's about giving a man a light?"

"He wasn't born idle," Betty commented, "he had to work hard to get like it."

Being on his feet, Ballinger walked to where Mark sat and leaned forward to offer a lit match. Out shot Mark's left hand and an instant later the detective felt his Webley slide from the holster.

"Now there's something we never thought of in time," Mark said, offering the gun butt forward to its owner.

Everybody realized the implications of what they had just seen. If Mark could take the gun with such ease, so could a prisoner.

"I never had that trouble," Dusty answered. "But an Army Colt's too long in the barrel for it to work."

"It's a chance in a thousand of anybody else doing it," Ballinger remarked.

"In this game it doesn't pay to take even such long odds," Dusty replied. "I'm beginning to think a cross-draw's no good for you, Ed."

"That'll please Joe Gaylin," Betty commented dryly. "Look, Ed, change the holster to the right side and I'll see if I can mark where to alter the loop. I can do that."

Changing the holster to the right side had the effect of tilting the butt forward and the barrel to the rear in a manner which looked unusual. So much so that, although the holster felt quite comfortable, Ballinger doubted if it would perform its functions. His hand went up, closed on the butt of the gun. In doing so he lowered his right shoulder slightly and scooped the gun out in a circular motion which brought it almost into a firing line before he could stop it.

"Hold it, Ed!" Dusty yelled, coming to his feet and spraying tobacco from the paper into which he poured it. "Do that again."

On replacing his gun and repeating the process, Ballinger was struck by the ease with which the gun came clear. Sheer blind chance had led them to the best method of carrying a short-barrelled revolver when concealment was necessary, but speed of withdrawal required.

Eagerly the Texans gathered around Ballinger and gave their views on his best way of handling his new draw. Long after midnight, Ole Devil's Japanese servant delivered a message to the effect that some folks wanted to sleep. By that time, after much experimentation, Ballinger knew that dropping his right shoulder allowed him to line the gun with more ease than when trying to thrust the shoulder forward. At last he felt he could imitate the smooth sweeping motion by which the Texans drew and shot.

Next morning Ballinger headed for the range, followed by the Texans, all eager to see if the new method stood the test of firing. After making a few practice draws, to ensure that he had the correct trigger-squeeze worked for the new method, Ballinger faced the man-shaped target, loaded and holstered his gun. Back dropped his shoulder, around circled the right hand to sweep the gun from leather. Flame tore from the stubby barrel and smoke momentarily hid the target. Not that

Ballinger needed to see it, the cheers of his friends told him that he had made a hit.

"Right in the belly!" Waco whooped.

Five more times, at a range of fifteen feet, Ballinger planted his bullets into the target. The holes varied, one down low, another in the centre of the throat, forming a rough line.

"Don't let that worry you, Ed," Mark commented. "Hit a feller in any of those places, even with a .41, and you'll put him down."

"Especially if you hit him down there," Waco went on, indicating the lowest hole and forgetting Betty's presence. "Man you'd sure ruin h—"

At which point Miss Hardin served notice of her presence by tossing the youngster over her shoulder, using one of the ju-jitsu throws Tommy Okasi taught her. Being something of a horse-master, Waco landed without hurting himself and started to rise.

The reason for Ballinger's improved accuracy did not take too much finding. Using the previous draw, he had to swing his gun across the width of the target and had only a limited distance in which to make a hit. With the new method, he lifted the gun upwards and had the length of torso and head on which to aim.

"It was as easy as that," Dusty groaned.

"They always are," answered Waco. "If you'd asked me be—" He dived away fast as Dusty swung in his direction.

"I'm not very fast," Ballinger remarked, thinking of the speed with which all his companions could draw and shoot.

"No," admitted Betty. "But you're hitting the target. They do say that speed's fine, but accuracy's final."

The speed came, slowly and gradually as the days rolled by. Having mastered the basic problem, Ballinger began to build up his new skill. Not only did he increase speed on the draw, but he also worked out other problems. Under Dusty's instruction, the detective learned how to get distance and accuracy from the Webley. Trial and error taught Ballinger how to sway his body so as to swing aside the jacket he would wear back home, leaving free access to the gun's butt. And always there was reaction training. From waking in the morning to going to bed at night, Ballinger wore his gun. At any moment a shout of 'Draw!' might come. On hearing the word, Ballinger snapped into action, shoulder dropping, hand sweeping out his gun.

Then on Wednesday of the third week, in one of his comparison tests working in competition with Red Blaze, the crack of the Webley sounded clearly ahead of the deeper bark of the Texan's Army Colt.

"You shaded me, Ed," Red announced delightedly. "Man, you're getting real fast."

"Will I be fast enough when the time comes?" Ballinger replied.

CHAPTER THIRTEEN

Draw!

Entering the big house from a practice session on the range shortly before sundown on Thursday evening, Ballinger found Betty Hardin in a blistering humor. An urgent matter had taken Dusty and all the floating outfit on to the range and she had to go into town. Not that Betty feared to ride the range alone, but she liked company and had some work that required male assistance.

"Find me a horse and I'll come along," Ballinger offered. "I feel like a change and haven't seen Hondo since Monday."

Over the past days Ballinger had seen much of Hondo Fog and revised many of his preconceived ideas. He knew that not all Western lawmen were ignorant hicks and admitted that the sheriff of Rio Hondo County could teach him a thing or two about practical law enforcement. In addition to learning of any new developments John County way, Ballinger liked to listen to Hondo talk about other Western lawmen and hear of the leading lights of the Texas Rangers, shrewd, capable men in whose service Hondo's second son, Danny, lost his life.*

"Come down to the corral," Betty said. "I'll pick you a horse."

* Danny Fog's story is told in *The Cow Thieves* and *A Town Called Yellowdog*.

"I just bet you will," grinned Ballinger, thinking of how he had been landed on a pretty wild mount shortly after his arrival.

"Don't worry," Betty smiled. "I haven't time to fool around like that."

Donning his jacket, and loading his Webley – the reaction training around the house meant that he could not keep bullets in the chambers when indoors – Ballinger went along to the corral and saddled the horse Betty caught for him. The ride to town passed uneventfully and on arrival they found that most of the businesses on the main street had already closed for the night. No lights showed at the sheriff's office for Hondo and his one paid deputy had left town to watch a trail along which a badly-wanted outlaw might be making a run for the border country. However the saloon was open, its batwing doors and windows glowing a welcome.

So engrossed in conversation were Betty and Ballinger, that neither noticed a man seated in the saloon by one of the windows. The man saw them, stiffened in his seat and peered through the window as they passed through its circle of light. Coming to his feet, the man threw a word to his companion and left the room. Outside, he followed the girl and Ballinger at a distance and watched as they took their horses around the rear of the jail to be left in the civic pound. Having seen that, the man turned and hurried back to the saloon.

Betty's business took a couple of hours and involved visiting various kinfolk. At last it ended and she walked with Ballinger towards the civic pound.

"I tell you, Ed," Betty said. "Aunt Martha's the talkingest woman—"

At which point her words ended abruptly as she became aware of the presence of a tall man in range clothes standing at the far end of the pound's fence. Even then Betty might not have thought anything, but a faint footfall sounded behind her. Two hands gripped Betty by the arms, jerking her backwards and away from the detective's side.

"Ed!" she screamed, and in that instant realized that the detective might not recognize the danger in time. There was only one thing that might work. "Draw!"

Already Ballinger had sensed danger. Something in the way the other man moved alerted the detective. He saw the other's hand start to move hipwards. Then Betty's second word reached him and triggered off what had become an almost automatic reaction. Without conscious direction on his part, Ballinger's right hand swept back to the Webley's butt. Given time to think, Ballinger might have hesitated and failed to respond with the necessary speed. Almost before he realized it, the Webley came out, barked and kicked against palm. For a moment the muzzle-blast blinded him. He heard the deeper crash of the other man's revolver merging with the sound of a close-passing bullet. The wisdom of selecting the Webley showed at that moment. If he had been using his Smith and Wesson, Ballinger would have died, but the .41 calibre bullet packed enough shock-power on impact to knock the other man off balance and caused his returning lead to miss the detective.

Having done what she could to save Ballinger, Betty gave thought to freeing herself from the man behind her. Back lashed her foot, its spurred heel driving into the man's leg. Pain caused his grip to relax and lose his hold with his left hand. Stepping back towards her assailant, Betty drove her free elbow savagely into his solar plexus. Although he grunted, the man still retained his hold. Like a flash the girl pivoted, swinging her body around the man's. Again she lashed out with her elbow, sending it with agonizing force into the man's kidney region. Snarling in a mixture of pain and fury, the man released and thrust Betty aside. Whatever his next action might have been, he changed his mind. Without a backward glance, he turned and fled as doors in surrounding buildings burst open.

Betty made no attempt to follow the man. While her knowledge of ju-jitsu and karate gave her an advantage she knew better than try to tangle with an armed, desperate man unless forced by sheer necessity. The man did not intend to resume his attentions, and a moment later hooves drummed then faded off rapidly, telling her that he was not coming back.

"Are you all right, Ed?" she asked, turning and seeing, with relief, that the detective was still standing.

"I - I reckon so," he replied, his voice hoarse, strained and unnatural.

Knowing the reason for it, Betty made no comment on how Ballinger's voice sounded. No man found his first killing easy and at that moment Ballinger must feel almost ready to fetch up. Moving forward, the girl halted at the detective's side. Lanterns gleamed as men approached to investigate the shooting.

"It was him or you, Ed," she said. "Don't ever forget it."

Having experience in similar situations, the approaching men identified themselves and made sure they could approach in safety before coming too close. The time taken for that allowed Ballinger to regain enough of his control and look natural before the men came up.

"Best see who he is," one man suggested, after Betty told what had happened.

A lantern's light showed a tall man wearing range clothes. Close to his right hand lay a smoking Army Colt. Ballinger's bullet had struck the man in the left side of his chest, killing him almost instantly.

"You know him, friend?" the bartender asked, looking at Ballinger.

"Never saw him before," the detective answered.

"He was in the bar earlier. Him and another feller," the bartender went on. "His pard left in a hurry, come back about ten minutes later. They had a couple of drinks and pulled out."

"Where's the other one now?" asked Ballinger.

"He pulled out in a hurry," Betty replied. "Went off to the west."

"What did he look like, mister?" the detective inquired, turning to the bartender. "He wouldn't've been a city man, would he?"

"Wore range clothes, but his hat didn't sit right for a westerner. I put him down as being like his pard. A hired gun, not a good one at that."

"Think they might have been from Jack City and looking for you, Ed?" asked Betty.

"Why else would they be here?"

"After horses, or fixing to rob us."

"It could be," he admitted. "I can't remember seeing this one in Jack City. Was the other headed that way when he left town?"

"Not unless he aimed to swing back in a big circle and hit the stage trail on the east of town," the girl replied. "I'll ask Uncle Jubal to take care of things here, Ed. The sooner we tell Dusty what's happened, the better I'll like it."

With what to Ballinger seemed like a surprising lack of formality, the affair was turned over to the owner of the hardware store. Taking their horses, Betty and the detective rode back to the O.D. Connected. During the ride, they discussed the incident and decided that robbery might be counted, but was less likely than an attempt on Ballinger's life by a couple of Jack City men either looking for him, or who came on him by chance. After some thought, Ballinger was inclined to go for the latter theory.

On returning to the ranch, Ballinger left his horse in the corral while Betty took her mount to the stables which housed the personal stock of the floating outfit. She joined the detective with news that, although Dusty,

Mark, Waco and Red were still out on the range, the Kid had returned. On reaching the house, they found the Kid, trail-dirty and tired, eating a meal in the dining-room.

"Went off fine," he replied to Betty's question about his mission. "I'm fixing to go into John County comes morning."

"Dusty won't be back," Betty replied. "I could send out and ask him if he can spare Waco."

"Let me come with you, Lon," Ballinger suggested.

For a moment the Kid hesitated, then reached a decision. He had already heard of the detective's progress in the matter of handling a gun and did not worry on that score. However the trip into John County called for more than gun-savvy.

"It'll be rough, Ed," he warned. "I'm riding a relay, two horses, to make time. If you can handle it, come along."

"I reckon I can manage," grinned the detective.

"How're you with a rifle?"

"Can hit what I aim at, sometimes. But I'll be wearing the Webley."

"We might run into a fight," the Kid pointed out. "If you're not *real* sure of your aim, take a ten-gauge instead of a rifle. Buckshot's a mighty convincing argument."

So it was decided. Next morning early, Ballinger slipped a ten-gauge, two-barrelled shotgun into the boot of one of his relays' saddle. Each man had two saddled horses, although the Kid did not take along his magnificent white stallion as it had been hard pushed bringing him from the Comanche reservation.

The ride lasted all day and covered sixty miles, but brought nothing exciting. Towards nightfall the Kid found a small stream which offered both water and shelter from prying eyes; on its bank they made camp. While Ballinger cared for the horses, his companion disappeared into the bushes to return some time later carrying two plump prairie chickens and a large ball of what appeared to be mud. Requesting that Ballinger pluck out the birds, the Kid busied himself digging a hole into which he buried the ball of mud, then he built a fire on the place.

While caring for the horses, Ballinger discovered how inadequate their food supply appeared to be. Apart from some strips of jerked meat, nutritious but unappetizing in appearance, coffee, milk and sugar, the Kid had brought nothing along. Not that Ballinger needed to worry on that score. From his early days, the Kid had learned to live off the land. That night Ballinger fed well on prairie chicken, which had been roasted on a green twig, and some roots the Kid produced.

"I'm sure living better than when I was with Red," the detective commented. "How'd you get those birds?"

"Just something I learned from Grandpappy Long Walker's lodge brothers," the Kid replied. "Anyways, Red went to the wrong kind of school. He only learned fool things like reading, writing and stuff."

Tired by the day's hard ride Ballinger slept well and when he woke in the grey light of dawn found the Kid already afoot. Crouching by the embers of the fire, the Kid dug up the now hard-baked ball of mud he buried the previous night. On cracking the mud, he exposed the body of a cooked turkey, its feathers removed with the mud covering.

"You should have woke me," Ballinger said, seeing that everything, apart from his bed roll, was ready for travel.

"Wasn't much to do," the Kid replied. "I wanted the fire out afore daylight so its smoke doesn't get seen. Come and eat."

After breakfast on turkey, which Ballinger swore tasted better than any bought in flash Chicago hotels, they resumed their journey. The country through which they travelled was broken, hilly, and wood covered. Once a small bunch of white-tail deer scattered before them; later Ballinger had the rare treat of seeing a cougar streak off into the trees.

Shortly after nine o'clock, the Kid brought his horses to a halt. Turning his head he sniffed the breeze like a redbone hound hitting coon scent.

"Smell it, Ed?" he asked.

"No," Ballinger replied after repeating the Kid's actions.

"We'll just ride up-wind a piece, see how you get on then."

After riding into the breeze for about two hundred yards, Ballinger caught the faint smell of burning wood and something else he could not put a name to, but which seemed vaguely familiar.

"That's a whisky-still boiling," the Kid explained, when the detective announced his discovery. "Be the Cutlers', I reckon."

"Let's ride over and talk," Ballinger suggested.

"Wouldn't do no good. Pappy 'n' me never got on with them shiftless bunch."

"How about sneaking up on them and seeing what they're doing?"

"I *know* what they're doing," grunted the Kid. "Likewise, one of 'em's up there with a Kentucky rifle as long as a fence rail and drawing a bead on us. Don't let on we've seen him."

"That'll be easy – I haven't," replied Ballinger, scanning the land ahead.

"We'll just swing off to the right easy, so's not to spook him," the Kid said. "Don't reckon he'll shoot. Knows he can't drop me without you getting him afore he can reload; there's something I don't like about this though."

Without saying another word, the Kid started his

horse moving again, turning it at an angle away from where he knew cold eyes watched him. Ballinger followed on the dark youngster's heels, but not until they had covered almost two miles did he find a chance to ask about the Kid's last words.

"I know them Cutlers. They're not lazy, they're plumb bone idle. Never thought to see one of 'em out of bed this early in the morning nor using a still so long after daylight come. It's not their way at all."

"What d'ya reckon's behind it?"

"I don't know, and that's for sure. Maybe we'll get us some answers down that ways a piece. Ole Wilkie Farrel used to do business with pappy in the old days. Only one thing though, Ed—"

"Yes?"

"Leave all the talking to me. Those hill-folks don't cotton none to strangers and get mighty close-mouthed."

The warning was not given in haste, for they covered almost three more miles without any sign of the Kid's friend. Riding through the wooded, sloping land which all looked alike to Ballinger, the Kid firmly remarked that the Farrel cabin lay beyond the next rim.

On reaching the head of the slope, the Kid brought his horses to a halt and a low exclamation burst from his lips. Ballinger stopped at the Kid's side and looked at the shattered ruin of a cabin in the centre of a small clearing. Just outside the door sprawled the body of a tall, white-haired old man clad only in a pair of long red flannel underpants, a Kentucky rifle scant inches from his fingers. Just ahead of the old man lay the body of a big, gaunt bluetick hound.

"What happened?" asked Ballinger.

"Damned if I know," growled the Kid. "We'll just ride in a mite closer, leave the hosses and look around some."

At the edge of the trees, both men dismounted and

left their horses. The Kid drew his rifle before walking out into the clearing and staring with savage concentration at the ground.

"It was no accident," Ballinger stated, as they approached the dead dog.

"Sure wasn't," agreed the Kid. "Somebody put a bullet into ole Sam here as he went for them. Just stop right there, Ed, while I take a look around."

For a moment Ballinger thought of objecting. Back in Chicago he had investigated more than one murder and felt that he could teach his companion a thing or two in that line. Then suddenly he realized how isolated he felt. He had none of the aids available in the city. In Chicago, even should the murder occur in one of the city's parks, there were always people about whom one might question; a doctor who would estimate the time of death; such scientific aids as then in use could be brought in; here, nothing. The nearest neighbor's place lay some five miles away. Ballinger had no idea how to start the investigation. So he stood still and watched the Kid.

Moving forward, eyes fixed on the ground, the Kid circled the dog's body. He came to a halt, dropped to one knee so as to study the grass ahead of him more closely, then rose and continued his examination.

"Come ahead, Ed," the Kid finally called. "Keep over to the right there."

On his way to join the Kid, Ballinger halted by the old man's body and looked down. A bullet had caught the centre of the white head, shattering out of the rear. Bending down, Ballinger touched the cold flesh, gently trying to move one arm. At last he felt that he might have something to add to the Kid's sum of knowledge, but waited for the other to speak.

"Best look inside," growled the Kid. "Wilkie was married and had two boys."

He forced his way through the ruined door and

looked at the wreck of torn, fallen timbers, then moved out again.

"Well?" asked Ballinger.

"They were inside. Still in bed," the Kid replied. "Three fellers came out of the trees over thatways just afore full daylight this morning. That ole Sam dog started bellowing and Wilkie let him out, came out with his rifle to see who was about. One of the three shot the dog, other dropped Wilkie and the third one threw either a bundle of dynamite, or a bomb, into the cabin."

"It was cold-blooded murder," Ballinger said. "If we only knew what the three looked like!"

"One was tall, maybe six-foot or more, lean and limped a mite. He threw the bomb. Feller at his right stood medium height, light built, he shot Sam with a Winchester. Other one was in between his pards in height, stocky and used a Spencer."

"How do you know all that?"

"It's all there, on the ground, Ed."

"You mean tracks?"

"Sure. Can tell from the way the grass's squashed down, length between the footprints, how tall and heavy the man who made 'em was. Feller who threw the bomb dragged his right foot a mite, that's how I know he limped. You didn't come near the line, so you haven't seen the two empty bullet cases they left behind."

During the Kid's absence, Ballinger had often heard the rest of the floating outfit boast of his ability at following a track. Yet it seemed incredible that the Kid could learn so much just by looking at the ground. Then Ballinger realized that his own estimation of the time of death, based on the stiffness of the body's limbs, coincided with that of the Kid. Being a sensible man, Ballinger admitted that he stood in the presence of a master and waited for the next move.

"We'll take after them and see where they went," the

Kid said. "Go get the hosses, Ed, I'll see where they went. Keep off the clearing though. Hondo might want to look it over."

By the time Ballinger had collected the horses and located his companion, the Kid produced a further example of his tracking and sign-reading skill. He stated that the tall man rode a bay mare, the middle one a roan and the shortest a sorrel, both geldings, and also that they had half-a-dozen pack horses along.

Given so large a party, Ballinger could see plenty of signs of their passage, but nothing to tell him how the Kid learned such detailed information. However such was Ballinger's faith in the dark young man at his side, that he raised no objections and put himself in the other's hands.

"They're not headed for either town or Reckharts' place," the Kid stated. "Fact being, they're making for – get off the trail fast, Ed, and keep the horses quiet."

Ballinger obeyed immediately and without question. Swinging his horses, he headed them into the trees and followed the Kid for some yards away from the trail. Dismounting, they fastened their horses to the bushes and then the Kid made sure that the animals would be hidden from sight. Rifle in hand, he nodded to Ballinger's shotgun in an unmistakable gesture. Taking the shotgun from its boot, Ballinger drew its hammers back to full cock, a good point that the Kid conceded to him. With his long arm in hand, Ballinger followed the Kid to halt behind a lusty cottonwood on the edge of the narrow winding trail they had followed.

A faint sound came to Ballinger's ears and he wondered what caused the Kid to make the moves just completed. Nearer came the sound and Ballinger realized it was several horses' hooves thudding, mingled with men talking. Yet he could not help marvelling that the Kid heard the approaching party so much earlier.

Before Ballinger could think more on the phenomenon, the first rider came into sight. A tall man in range clothes, lean, hard looking and riding a bay. Then the rest of the party, each leading two loaded pack animals, came into sight. One was much shorter than the bay's rider and afork a sorrel; the other came between them in height, had a stock build and rode a roan.

CHAPTER FOURTEEN

A Simple Piece of Interrogation

Even as the trio approached, Ballinger realized that the Kid had been very accurate in his description. Yet how the dark younster knew was beyond Ballinger's imagination.

Suddenly the Kid moved. In complete silence he left his hiding place and landed on the trail before the approaching trio. Imagining himself partially hidden behind the lean man, the stocky jasper reached towards his gun. He presented only a small target, but sufficient for a man of the Kid's superlative ability in the use of the rifle. From hip high the old "yellowboy" crashed, its flat-nosed .44 Henry bullet tearing by the lean man, stirring his sieeve in passing, to drive home under the other's right eye, up through the brain and out of the top of the head.

At which point Ballinger made his presence known. "Hold it!" he yelled, the ten-gauge snuggling against his shoulder and directing its yawning muzzles at the remaining pair of men. Thereby ended all opposition. No man in any state of mind argued when covered by a double-barrelled ten-gauge at a range where its deadly nine-buckshot load would just be spread body-wide.

"Get down slow and easy!" ordered the Kid, his rifle's lever blurring and flicking clear an empty case to replace it with another loaded bullet.

"We work for Harte," warned the taller man.

"Likely," growled the Kid, and gestured gently with the Winchester.

Slowly, making sure that they kept both hands in plain sight, the two men began to dismount. They accomplished it despite the restive manner in which the pack animals moved. A pack suddenly came loose and crashed to the ground. Glass shattered and the raw, acrid stench of spilled whisky rose as liquid gushed out on to the ground.

"Keep 'em covered, Ed," ordered the Kid. "Shed those gunbelts and come this way."

Using the left hand only, each man unbuckled his gunbelt and tossed it aside. They could read the signs and knew that any attempt to disobey at that moment would be instantly fatal. After ordering the disarmed pair to walk clear of their horses, the Kid told Ballinger to put aside his shotgun and hog-tie the two men.

A later innovation to Ballinger's gunbelt had been to install a pouch in which to carry his handcuffs. After putting his gun behind the tree, Ballinger took out the cuffs and advanced. Part of his training while awaiting the Kid's return had been in the matter of securing prisoners. So he knew enough to stay out of the Kid's line of fire, and not go to where the men might lay hands on him and use him as a shield.

Making the tall man extend his arms shoulder high, Ballinger stood back and clamped home the handcuffs. The detective could claim to be something of a student of human nature and knew that, of the two, the taller was the more dangerous. So he used the handcuffs to nullify that one's menace before giving thought to the other.

"How about him?" asked Ballinger, realizing that the Kid did not carry handcuffs.

"We're going to ask him some questions," the Kid replied.

That seemed logical to Ballinger. In fact it might have been more to the point *before* the third man died.

Ballinger knew that he had only the Kid's word that three men answering the trio's description killed the family. Certainly he could not see a jury accepting such flimsy evidence. In the 1870's, law enforcement officers frequently used rough tactics to extract confessions and Ballinger knew a trick or two which worked, given time. He doubted if the Kid possessed such technical knowledge.

"Why'd you kill the Farrels?" Ballinger barked, retrieving his shotgun.

"I don't know what you mean," answered the lean man.

One look told Ballinger that the taller man would be a hard nut to crack. If either broke, it would be the other. Both appeared to have been sampling the whisky in the packs, yet the Kid's sudden appearance and the death of their companion had sobered them. Now a hint of fear crept to the smaller man's face. He would be the one to work on.

Even before Ballinger reached that conclusion, the Kid acted. As in everything he did, the dark youngster took the simplest way. Leaning his rifle behind a tree, he took out his bowie knife, stepped forward, caught the smaller man by the shirt front and thrust him against the tree's rough trunk.

"We want answers," the Kid growled, resting the tip of his knife under the man's chin. "And you're going to give them to us."

"Shut your yap!" roared the taller man, lunging forward.

Like a flash, the Kid pivoted and lashed his right arm around – the left retaining its hold of the smaller man's shirt. The sun glinted on razor-sharp steel as it rushed around to meet the oncoming man. They came together, meeting with a savage impact. The man cried out in pain, spun around and his hands went to his face; something red ran down his cheek from under the exploring fingers.

For a moment Ballinger thought that the Kid's knife had laid open the lean man's face. So it had, but the brass quillon of the crossguard inflicted the damage and not the eleven and a half inch blade. Love of humanity did not prompt the Kid's lenient action. He figured they could make the smaller man talk, but if the cuss should prove tougher than he imagined, he wanted the other able to speak; a thing difficult to do with one's face split wide open from eye to chin.

Ignoring the taller man, the Kid swung back to his weakly struggling captive. Fear showed in the man's eyes as he stared from his companion's bleeding face to the wicked clip-pointed blade forged by the Arkansas master James Black – the man who produced the prototype for Jim Bowie.

"Tell it all," growled the Kid. "*Pronto*, afore I start peeling the skin off your face in inches."

Ballinger wondered if the Kid intended to carry out his threat and decided that it was entirely possible. In which case the detective tried to decide what his attitude should be. While living in a rough age Ballinger tried to be as human as possible. He doubted if he could stand by and watch the man, no matter how the other might deserve it for his part in the slaughter of the whole family. He did not need to worry. If Ballinger wondered whether the Kid aimed to carry out the threat, the small man, born and raised on the Western plains, held no such doubts. Recalling the story of Dusty Fog's ears,* the man did not for a moment believe the Kid made idle threats.

"It was Brack there who threw the bomb!" he howled, indicating the tall man. "And Wilson shot the old man. All I did was drop the dog. I had to, it come out of that cabin like a bear coming out of a hole."

"Why'd you go after old Wilkie?" growled the Kid.

"He wouldn't sell to us no more and was fixing to

* Told in *A Town Called Yellowdog*

gather the other 'shiners to fight against us. So the boss sent us up here to throw a scare into him – that's all I thought we was going to do!'' The man's face twisted into pleading lines as he watched the Comanche-mean face for some hint of belief and saw none. ''I thought we meant to warn him, that's all. Only Brack had one of them Ketchum hand bombs we used in the war. I dropped the dawg, had to, it meant to get us. The old-timer come out with that Kentucky long gun and Wilson shot him. Then Brack threw that bomb.''

''Who's the boss?'' Ballinger asked.

''Harte, we call him *Hombre Grande*.''

''Which is Big Man in English,'' the Kid translated. ''So Harte sent you out here to throw a scare into old Wilkie, huh?''

''Sure,'' the man agreed. ''That's all.''

The story came rushing out. On his arrival in John County, Reckharts gathered in all the moonshiners and arranged to sell their produce. Backed by his hired guns, using force to emphasize his determination, the Big Man made every still owner in the county work for him. By bottling the home-brewed liquor under the Dennison's Old Whipping Post label, and selling it at a lower price than the genuine article, Reckharts hoped to evade trouble with the Government agents responsible for collecting the tax imposed on legitimate whisky distillers. Unscrupulous saloon owners accepted the offer of a cheap supply of whisky and Reckharts hoped that Dennisons would believe that for some reason the sales of their product had fallen off. Any salesman who visited one of Reckharts' customers would be shown unopened bottles as a reason for not ordering further stock.

At first all went well, but business boomed and more of the fake stock was needed. Reckharts began to demand a bigger output and struck a snag. While they now made more money than ever before, the moonshiners objected to the extra work forced upon them by the Big Man's increased demands. Instead of leisurely making enough corn liquor for their own use and small local sales – a matter of a few hours' work a couple of nights a week – the moonshiners found themselves kept at labor almost twenty-four hours a day. Never willing to accept steady work that cut in on their hunting and lazing-time, the moonshiners objected. However they made no concerted moves, lacking a leader. Reckharts knew it would be only a matter of time before such a leader rose and sensed that Wilkie Farrel would be that man. So the Big Man prepared to nullify the menace. Hearing that the old-timer flatly refused to work any more, Reckharts sent the three men to deal with him.

So interested had Ballinger become, that he let his attention drift away from Brack. Suddenly the lean man moved. Down dropped his shoulder and he charged into the detective, knocking Ballinger off balance. For a man with a slight limp, Brack could move fast. Down shot his bloody hands, closing on the shotgun and tearing it from Ballinger's grasp.

Ballinger's brains screamed the word 'Draw!' and his reactions took over once again without conscious effort. While still staggering and an instant after losing the shotgun, his subconscious gave the order and his right hand stubbed to the Webley's butt. Out came the snub-nosed revolver, even as the barrels of the ten-gauge turned towards him. Ballinger fired, triggering off a shot and sending the bullet into the lean man. Although hit, Brack did not let loose his hold on the shotgun.

Hearing the disturbance, the Kid whirled, his knife flipping through the air to the left hand so as to leave the right free to draw the old Dragoon. At first the Kid thought his services might not be needed. Then he saw Ballinger fail to observe a basic precaution when dealing with such a situation. Hit in the chest, Brack retained his hold of the shotgun and tried to complete swinging it into line on the detective.

Ballinger had seen his bullet hit Brack and held his

fire, expecting the man to go down. Not so the Kid. Flame belched from the Dragoon's barrel and a soft lead, round ball – as opposed to the conical-shaped bullets Ballinger used – tore into Brack's body. Powered by a full forty grains of powder, the .44 bullet knocked Brack staggering and although the shotgun roared, its lethal charge missed the detective by inches.

Scared by the shots, the horses began to rear and pitch. Bottles crashed and shattered in the packs. Wilson's mount and its two pack horses went charging into the bushes, but Brack's mount stood fast. Although the small man's horse tried to bolt, its reins became tangled around its legs and brought it to a halt. The struggles of the scared pack horses tore all but one free and they burst wildly off through the surrounding woodland.

"Hold it!" Ballinger yelled, swinging his head towards their last living prisoner.

Spinning around, the Kid saw the small man had turned as if to make a dash for safety and freedom. Whipping back his left arm, the Kid brought it forward and threw his knife underhand. The man yelled as the big knife flashed before his eyes to sink quivering into the tree truck ahead of him. Any thoughts of escape he might have nursed died immediately.

"Didn't get you with any of the buckshot, did he, Ed?" asked the Kid, retrieving his knife.

"Missed me clean," the detective replied, taking up the shotgun.

"Didn't Dusty tell you always to shoot again if the feller you've hit don't drop his gun?"

"Sure."

"You want to mind that next time. Maybe he couldn't't've lasted long enough to get that scatter around far enough to hit you. But you'd sure been sore if he had."

The detective sucked in a deep breath and nodded. During his training, he had often been told of how he should conduct himself in a gunfight. The matter of shooting again should his opponent not drop his gun had been one point stressed many times. Ballinger could now see the reason for the warning and stored it away in his memory.

"What now?" he asked.

"Those hosses'll head back to the Reckharts place, likely men'll be out looking for this bunch," the Kid replied. "We've got all we came after. I'd say we head back to Polveroso and set it afore Hondo and Dusty."

"And the bodies?"

"Leave them lie. We can't take 'em with us. The sooner we get back to Polveroso, the quicker we can start thinking about taking Reckharts. I reckon that's what you want to do."

"I reckon you're right at that," the detective agreed. "We'll be taking this feller in."

"As long as he keeps up with us. First time he tries to slow us down, he won't be coming along any more. He knew they'd come out here to kill Wilkie Farrel."

"I – I didn't—" the man yelped.

"Don't lie to me," growled the Kid. "You know old Wilkie didn't scare worth a damn. The only way you'd make him change his mind was kill him. Now go get those two hosses and be ready to ride."

"I'll take his rifle," Ballinger remarked, walking towards the horses. "It might be handy as evidence. Pity his pard's went though."

"What kind of gun did Wilson have in his boot, *hombre*?" asked the Kid.

"A Spencer carbine."

"And this's a Winchester, Lon," Ballinger commented, drawing the man's rifle. "You called everything just right."

"That don't surprise me any at all," answered the Kid cheerfully. "Turn loose that pack hoss, Ed."

"We could use its load as evidence," the detective objected. "It establishes a motive for the murders."

"All right, bring the fool critter along. It won't slow us down much."

"Why'd they take so long after the killing in coming back with this whisky do you reckon, Lon?"

"We've got a gént who *knows* the answers," the Kid replied.

"The old feller'd changed where his still had been hid," the man explained. "It took us time to find it and load up the stuff he'd already made and bottled."

"And if that's all you want to know, let's ride," drawled the Kid. "We want a good head start afore those pack horses find their way to the ranch and start all kinds of evil thoughts going in Reckharts' head. One way and another, he's not going to like us for what we've done and know."

"That's for sure," agreed Ballinger. "Let's go."

Leaving the bodies where they had fallen, Ballinger, the Kid and their prisoner took to their horses and headed west. Although Ballinger admitted to himself that he was hopelessly lost, the Kid never hesitated. They took a shorter, more direct route than on the way out and pushed the horses hard. Nor did the prisoner make any attempt to slow them down. He knew the Kid by reputation and nothing so far seen led him to assume that the reputation was false.

Nightfall found them camped on the border of Rio Hondo and John Counties. Although not fastened in any way, the prisoner made no attempt to escape during the hours of darkness. Having spent some of his life in or around the Mexican border country, he knew the old Spanish custom of allowing a prisoner the opportunity to escape, then shooting him during the attempt. The Kid had strong links with Mexico and undoubtedly knew of *ley fuega*; so the prisoner did not intend to present an opportunity to put it into practice.

At dawn the three men rode on, crossing the great ranges of the O.D. Connected. Good luck favored them and they met up with a trio of the ranch's hands out gathering cattle. On the Kid's orders, the trio left their work and separated. The first struck to the north with a message for Red Blaze's brothers at their Double B ranch. Heading south, the second carried news of the Kid's mission to where Dusty and the floating outfit worked. Going to the west at a gallop, the last of the trio made for the O.D. Connected's house to pass word to Ole Devil Hardin. Having made his arrangements, the Kid pointed his leg-weary horses in the direction of Polveroso.

The results of the messages showed during the remainder of the day. Of the O.D. Connected's crew of eighteen cowhands, ten and the floating outfit came in. Towards evening, Pete Blaze reached town accompanied by nine of the Double B crew. Some dozen local citizens volunteered their services in the cause of Justice. Further help appeared when Captain Murat of Company 'G' rode in with a round dozen of his Texas Rangers. Hondo had telegraphed to Murat on hearing of the Kid's return and departure for John County. With such a force at his disposal, Hondo figured he ought to be able to handle Reckharts' hired guns.

Ballinger sat in the sheriff's office that evening and watched the plans being made. Clearly every man present had been on such expeditions before, as showed in the way they settled into the business of organization. Having helped plan more than one raid, Ballinger could not help admiring the way Hondo made his arrangements. First thing to be settled was who commanded the whole affair. The Rio Hondo men accepted without question that their sheriff should do so and Murat gave his agreement. While the cowhands might respect a Ranger, they would be more likely to work willingly under the guidance of a local man.

Once put in sole command, Hondo wasted no time in organizing. Again Ballinger found himself feeling some awe. Fixing a raid of twenty or so men in Chicago paled to nothing compared with organizing a posse of over

fifty, especially when one considered that they had to
cover almost seventy miles, much of it through hostile
territory. This latter aspect caused the Texans less concern than it did Ballinger. Most of them spent much of
their working life astride a horse and the prospect of a
long ride did not worry them. In addition almost all the
Rio Hondo men served in the Texas Light Cavalry
during the war; and not a few rode in Dusty's Company
'C' on its numerous strikes deep into Yankee-held
territory.* The thought of a good fight as a change from
the routine work on the ranges made up for their having
to face a gruelling seventy-mile ride at high speed.

Once into John County, the party would travel as in
hostile country, with scouts out ahead, on the flanks
and in the rear. The services of the Ysabel Kid would
not be available for that duty. He had the task of
rounding up as many of the moonshiners as he could so
they might lend their skilled sighting eyes to the task of
taking the Reckharts ranch and town.

At last all was arranged and the rank and file of the
posse informed of their duties, then told to make themselves comfortable for the night. Dawn found the men
in their saddles and riding towards John County. With
the Texans rode Ed Ballinger, determined to finish the
mission which brought him from Chicago.

* One such raid is recorded in *The Colt And The Sabre*.

CHAPTER FIFTEEN

Reckharts' Luck

"I can't say that I like this," Dusty Fog stated, as he walked leading his paint stallion between his father and Ballinger. "We're going to hit the Reckharts place at noon."

"Looks that way," Hondo admitted. "Only there's not much we can do about it, Dusty."

"Might stay out here and move in after dark," Murat, walking at Ballinger's left side, suggested. "We've seen no sign of Reckharts' men so far."

"That worries me," Dusty drawled. "The pack horses ought to have got back to the spread by now."

At that moment, Waco out front as scout halted, reaching for the butt of his rifle. Although he drew the Winchester, the youngster made no attempt to use it. Instead he turned and signalled to the main body.

"Halt!" Hondo called, and swung into his saddle. "Let's take a look, Dusty. Coming, Ed, Jules?"

Ballinger and Murat mounted, riding forward with Dusty and Hondo to where Waco stood waiting. On reaching the youngster, the men looked down a slope to where a wagon stood. Beyond the wagon two horses, one carrying double, were galloped away by their riders.

"Sorry, Hondo," Waco said. "That feller on his own saw me afore I saw him. Must have laid up and watched. He lit out real *pronto*; gathered his *amigos* and went like the devil after a yearling."

"He likely heard us coming boy," Dusty put in. "This many men make a fair piece of noise. Cover me, I'm going down there. It could be a trap."

"Let me go then," Waco put in. "I let him get away."

Without waiting for refusal or permission, the youngster vaulted to his big paint stallion and rode down the slope. Although he carried his rifle ready for use, he did not need it. Reaching the wagon, he circled it, then rode around to the rear. The tarpaulin cover of the wagon was tied down at the back and front in a manner which prevented the load from being seen. Taking out his knife, Waco slit the lashing and dragged open the canvas. By the time Waco cleared a way into the wagon, the other men had come down to join him.

"Whisky," Waco stated from inside the wagon, after forcing open one of the boxes which formed the load, though the boxes read "Horse Liniment." "Dennison's Old Whipping Post."

"Wouldn't want folks to know what they're shipping," Hondo replied.

"Trouble being that they're running to the ranch," Murat commented, nodding towards the departing men who had handled the wagon. "Looks like we'll have to go on in now, like it or not."

"Take a point, Dusty," Hondo ordered. "See how the land lies. Go with him, Waco. Don't try to handle them, wait until we come up."

"Yo!" Dusty replied. "Wouldn't want to spoil your bunch's fun."

"Reckon they aim to make a fight, Dusty?" asked Waco, as they rode along the wagon trail down which the men departed.

"I'd be surprised as hell if they didn't," Dusty replied, drawing his Winchester carbine from its boot. "Only you and I aren't fixing to tie into them. All we have to do is ride along and see how tough a nut the posse has to crack."

In the days before Reckharts' arrival, Dusty had visited the ranch and knew where it lay. A mile after leaving the wagon, he gave the order to dismount. Leaving their horses standing range-tied, with reins trailing down free, the Texans darted forward on foot. They approached the head of a slope cautiously and flattened down before looking over.

The trail ran down the slope to before the front of the main house. Already men armed with rifles dashed about, selecting places from which to make a fight.

"I'd say that's a tolerable tough nut to crack, Dusty," Waco commented.

"Don't let on I said so, boy," drawled Dusty, "but you're right – for once."

Clearly whoever set up the ranch's buildings did so with an eye on possible defense against attack. The house might not be such an imposing structure as Reckharts' Streeterville mansion, but it looked strong enough. Built of wood and with two floors, the house would take some capturing, even without the rest of the layout. To the right of the house stood a large barn, on the left a store shack and in the rear several stationary wagons. The whole place looked more like some freight-hauling outfit's headquarters than a cattle spread. While the slopes and country around the buildings offered reasonable cover for an attacking force, each building covered and mutually supported the others. Reckharts appeared to run a big crew, enough to amply garrison each building. A couple of men headed to each wagon, clearly aiming to make their fight from the vehicles. More covered the two corrals, although most of the horses which the spread must keep were range-grazing some distance away.

"Stay on here and watch them," Dusty ordered, after studying the layout. "I'll go back and tell paw what we've seen."

Waco nodded and settled down, his rifle resting on the ground. When Dusty's voice took on that grim note,

it did not pay to waste time asking questions. Studying
the buildings and their defences, Waco realized just how
hard it would be to take them. But such was his faith in
Dusty that the youngster did not doubt that the Rio
Hondo gun wizard would come up with an answer to the
problem.

Signalling the posse to halt, Hondo listened to
Dusty's description of the situation. They called in
the other leaders and, using a piece of earth scraped
level, Dusty drew a map of the area. Studying the detail, all the men realized just how hard a fight they
would have.

Before any plans could be made, the Kid made his appearance at the head of a good twenty rifle-toting John
County citizens. He had ridden a relay of three horses
into a mucksweat, but kept his huge white stallion for
future use. Bringing up the men to where Hondo stood,
the Kid stated that he guaranteed no legal proceedings
would be taken against any of them for moonshining.
Hondo agreed, he had no jurisdictional right to do
otherwise, and Captain Murat seconded the motion
with the proviso that the moonshiners went back to their
old ways as soon as Reckharts was driven out. This
having been their intention, the John County men
agreed and stated their willingness to follow Hondo's
orders in the forthcoming fighting.

While the details of the moonshiners' future were
being settled, Dusty solved a problem which had been
bothering him. The Cutler who had seen the Kid and
Ballinger followed them, watched the shooting of Brack
and Wilson, then gathered up all the escaped horses.
Reckharts' ranch crew did not know what orders
Brack's party received and thought nothing when the
trio failed to return; and the Big Man had been away on
business.

Swiftly Hondo gave his orders and sent men to ride
around and encircle the ranch buildings from a distance.

While waiting for the posse to take its position, the sheriff joined the floating outfit and looked down at the buildings.

"Maybe we could bring in that wagon and roll her down the track," Mark said. "It would plough straight into the main house. All that whisky would sure burn good and those timbers look awful dry."

"And with the main house gone, we could take the other places one at a time," Waco went on.

"Only it won't work," Dusty replied. "The moment we bring that wagon up here they'll know what we plan and shoot the horses."

"Take the hosses out and we'll push her over," Waco suggested.

"There's not much level ground to cover, boy," Dusty drawled. "But the men doing the pushing would be picked off by the flanking guns in the barn and store, even if they were behind the wagon."

"One man wouldn't," Mark said quietly. "He'd be right in the center and hid from both sides."

Ballinger had been in on the conference and put his say in. "One man couldn't start that wagon moving."

"Not start it, maybe," Mark agreed. "But once it started, I reckon I could keep it rolling as far as the head of the slope."

Looking at Mark's giant physique and thinking back to some of the feats of strength he had performed, Hondo knew that if any man could single-handedly keep the two-horse wagon moving, he was the one.

"It's worth a try," the sheriff said. "How do we make sure that the whisky takes fire?"

"Strip off the tarp, bundle it up and soak it well," Dusty answered. "Then get some of that grease-wood from back there on the slopes. Put them both up the front and set her off."

"Go to it then," Hondo ordered, as the sound of shots reached his ears.

Taking his paint, Waco galloped back to the whisky-wagon and returned with it at full speed. Dusty wasted no time in calling away some of the O.D. Connected hands and setting them to work. Swiftly eager hands stripped off the tarpaulin and cleared a space at the front of the wagon in which to make the fire. The wagon was drawn forward as far as possible before removing its team. Then Mark took his place in the centre of the rear and others of the men gathered around to help. Dusty struck and applied a match to the dried grass and grease-wood twigs which would take fire so easily. After ensuring that the flames caught, he sprang from the wagon and gave the order to push.

Hard shoving, aided by other men pulling on the wheel spokes, overcame the wagon's inertia and started it moving. Slowly it rolled forward, up the last few feet of the rim and on to the level land. Down below, the defenders saw what was happening and read the danger. Although the Kid and several selected riflemen threw lead downwards, they could not stop the opposition shooting at the wagon-pushers.

"Get clear!" Dusty yelled.

An instant later, one of the cowhands lost his hat to a rifle bullet and that brought about a hurried dash for safety. Then every eye went to where Mark Counter continued to push. Hands flat against the rear of the wagon, every muscle in his giant frame straining its utmost, the big blond fought to keep that wagon moving. Even though its wheels had been freshly greased, the wagon did not move easily. Mark's boots spiked into the ground, digging furrows in the hard-packed surface under the strain. Those boots had been made by Joe Gaylin, no lesser man could have assembled materials to take such punishing treatment and stay whole.

Down below, the rifles of the defenders raked the wagon. However none of the flanking guns could sight on the straining giant, but only by the narrowest of margins. Two men could not have stood side by side and avoided being seen.

Inch after inch, slowly but inexorably the wagon crept forward. Mark felt that his lungs would burst into flames as his heart pounded like a trip-hammer and sweat blinded him. Then a change came. The terrible weight began to ease and it became easier to keep the wagon moving.

"Get clear, Mark!" Dusty yelled, seeing the wagon tilt down the slope.

Words meant nothing to Mark at that moment. His legs continued to force forward and his hands to press against the tail-gate of the wagon. The final few steps were agony, before the wagon rolled forward under its own momentum. Feeling the tremendous weight leave him, Mark sank to his knees. At that moment the blond giant, spent and helpless after his exertions, was in the greatest peril of his life. Two things saved him: his exhaustion causing him to fall forward on to his face and the hail of lead sent down at the defenders and preventing a careful sight being taken on the helpless figure.

With ever-increasing speed the wagon raced down the slope. Fanned by the wind, the flames roared up and began to eat at the sun-baked timbers. A roaring blaze licked the air as the wagon careered down the slope and tore across the open land towards the front of the house. Although slowing, it still possessed enough momentum to mount the porch and smash into the front of the house. The impact pitched the cargo all ways, glass shattering, the whisky gushing out to feed and increase the fire. While buckets of water could have doused the blaze, using them would be impossible under the rifles of the posse.

Even as Mark recovered enough to wriggle back to safety, men started to leave the blazing house and dash for other cover. Ballinger did not use a rifle. Focusing a pair of powerful field-glasses, he watched the men leaving the building and hoped to see either Reckharts or Lash. At last the stream of departing men ended, and still without a sight of the men Ballinger had come so far to arrest. By that time, the house was blazing to such an extent that nobody could remain in it for much longer. So Ballinger kept the glasses trained.

"Over that way, Ed!" the Kid suddenly yelled, pointing to beyond the blazing house. "Two fellers watching us."

Bringing up the glasses, Ballinger swept the rim beyond that which the posse used in their circle around the building. He saw a wagon trail and on it two men who hurriedly turned their horses. Even though the men were over half a mile away, the detective recognized them.

"It's Reckharts and Lash!" he roared. "The bastard's done it again!"

Dusty had seen the distant shapes and wasted no time. "O.D. Connected! Get to your horses!" he yelled.

Knowing that of all the John County crowd Reckharts and Lash must be taken, Hondo raised no objections to his son's actions. The trail led to Jack City and once there Reckharts could find men to back his play. Dusty would need men to help bring Reckharts and Lash in and preferred to have his own ranch's crew backing him. Nor would the loss of the fifteen men make any serious difference to the posse at that stage of the proceedings.

Ballinger ran with the other men to where the horses waited. Mounting fast, the party swung around the line of attackers until they reached the Jack City trail and headed towards the town.

During the whole of the two-mile ride to Jack City, Dusty's party saw no sign of Reckharts and Lash. At last the town came into view, lying ahead of them. People walked the streets, a large bunch of horses stood hitched to the Tumbleweed's rail. Not what Dusty expected at all.

"Straight on in, boys," he ordered. "Only be ready for a trap."

"Either those folks are mighty brave, or they don't figure we'll be doing any shooting," Mark said, as they drew nearer.

Any Western crowd, knowing the nature of the cowhands' visit, ought to be hunting for cover. Yet, apart from a few curious glances, none of the people on the street showed any interest in the O.D. Connected's arrival. Music, talk and laughter blared from the Tumbleweed as the cowhands drew near. The Kid studied the line of horses, paying particular attention to the dinner-plate saddles each carried. Only one class of people went in for those large-horned rigs, and only one variety of that class were likely to be in Jack City.

"Mark, Waco, Lon, Red, Ed," Dusty said. "We're going in. Billy Jack, keep the boys out here. Happen there's some shooting, find holes and cover us as we leave."

"Yo!" answered the tall, gaunt, miserable looking cowhand who had ridden as Dusty's very able sergeant-major during the war.

Apparently the crowd in the saloon hoped to lull the Texans' suspicions by acting normally. Celebrating Mexicans formed the majority of the customers; well-dressed and armed men with money to spend. They sat around flirting with the girls; stood at the bar drinking; attempted to lick the house's percentage at various games of chance; but whatever they did, none paid the slightest attention as the batwing doors opened. The first person to give any sign proved to be the band's pianist. While thumping out a lively tune, he happened to glance at the doors. What he saw caused him to miss the correct keys, produce a jangling discord and then stop playing. Musician after musician stared towards

the door and forgot their work of entertaining the
customers. Then talk died down as every other eye went
to the six men who fanned across the main entrance.

"*Saludos*, Cuellar," the Kid greeted, addressing the
best-dressed man in the room; a man at whom all the
other Mexicans looked for guidance.

"*Cabrito*, is it not?" Ruis Cuellar inquired. "Do you
come in peace or war, *amigo*?"

"We're come for that feller you call Harte. Aim to
have him. How do you stand on it?"

"*El Hombre Grande* has put much business my way,
Cabrito."

"There're ten rifles outside, more 'case we need them
– and there's not a man here fast enough to stop us
leaving."

Slowly Cuellar ran his eyes over the six *Americanos
de Norte* facing him. During a long career as a border
smuggler, Cuellar had come to know gun fighting men
and could spot quality when he saw it. And, mister, he
saw it in large quantities before him. Every one of the
six, even the dude, showed he could handle a gun with
considerable skill; but that applied even more so to the
big blond Texan with the butt forward, bone-handled
Colts at his sides. There stood a man, a master in the art
of draw-and-shoot, one of the real top guns.

So, although the crowd contained a number of
pistoleros valients – men hired for their skill with a gun
and courage to use it—Cuellar gave a grave nod.

"What is a business acquaintance?" he said. "There
are always people who will buy my goods."

At which point Lighthouse made his biggest – and
final – mistake. Since coming West, he had developed
an intimacy with guns not possible to attain in the more
settled area of Chicago. Under the bar close to his hand
lay a sawed-off shotgun with which he had quelled more
than one hostile demonstration by disgruntled
customers. While not being entirely sure what the
Texans wanted, he recognized Ballinger and saw an

ideal opportunity to win his employer's approbation. With that thought in mind, he laid hold of the gun and started to swing it over the top of the counter.

Three-quarters of a second later Lighthouse's long-suffering wife became a widow.

Dusty's hands crossed even as Lighthouse started to raise the shotgun. Out came the matched Colts and the right-hand weapon cracked. Caught in the chest by Dusty's bullet, Lighthouse slammed back and struck the rear wall. Although the shotgun went off, its load of buckshot tore up into the roof.

At the first hint of trouble all Dusty's party acted correctly. First Mark, then Waco, followed by Ballinger and Red – one could not count the Kid as he gave thought only to his old "yellowboy" – produced their weapons. In just over a second after Lighthouse committed suicide, nine revolvers and a rifle covered the occupants of the room.

"Stand still!" Cuellar order in Spanish, then bowed in Dusty's direction. "I take no part in this, *señor*."

"*Gracias*." Dusty replied, and raised his voice. "Don't pee your pants, Billy Jack, there won't be any more bangs."

"I should think not too, for shame," came the reply in a shaky falsetto voice.

"Where's your boss?" Dusty asked, turning his attention to one of the saloon's employees.

"He headed for the spread a piece back, Cap'n."

"And didn't come back?"

"Never saw him."

"Where's his office?"

"That room at the side of the bar there, Cap'n."

"Waco, Ed," Dusty said. "Take it."

Watched by the crowd, Mark and Ballinger crossed the room. Raising his right leg, Mark delivered a kick which burst open the office door. Ballinger had practiced his next actions many times during his training. Swiftly he went into the room, darting from right to left the instant after Mark sent the door bursting inwards. Hot on his heels, going from left to right, Mark followed. They entered with guns in hands, ready to shoot, and found an empty room.

"Looks like they never came back, Dusty," Mark said, entering the barroom once more.

"You mean that *el Hombre Grande* knew of our danger and did not come to warn us?" asked Cuellar.

"That's just what he did," agreed the Kid.

"And I thought he had much courage, riding with us as we brought in the shipment."

"Rode with you, huh?"

"*Si, Cabrito.*"

"You still using the old Skull Crossing?"

"It is the best one in these parts."

"Let's go, Ed," the Kid said, his voice showing an unusual trace of emotion. "Turn these gents loose, Dusty."

"Sure," Dusty agreed. "You'll have a couple of hours, *Señor* Cuellar. Then the Rangers'll be here."

With that Dusty left the room. Already Ballinger and the Kid had mounted and Dusty learned that they did not want help. So he prepared to return to the ranch and tell Reckharts' men that their boss had deserted them.

CHAPTER SIXTEEN

Reckharts' Luck Runs Out

Sheer good fortune saved Reckharts and Lash from running into trouble at the ranch. On their return from accompanying Cuellar's smuggler train, they intended to ride straight to the ranch. Cuellar insisted on setting up the drinks and by the time the two men headed out of Jack City, the attack was just being launched.

On hearing the sound of shooting, Reckharts' first thought had been to run. Lash insisted that they first ride closer and check on how serious a threat there might be. If the attackers proved to be a disgruntled band of moonshiners, Lash figured on bringing in Cuellar's *pistoleros* and teaching the local citizens a lesson they would never forget.

The sight of the attacking force told Lash all he needed to know. Arriving just after the wagon crashed into the house, Lash knew that it would only be a matter of time before the defense crumbled.

"Let's go," he said. "We'd best head for Jack City and gather all the cash we can lay hands on, then get Cuellar to take us below the border."

"It'd be best," Reckharts agreed.

But the plan failed. Soon after, just as they passed over a rim, Lash looked back and saw the O.D. Connected men following in the distance. Guessing that the Texans intended to make for Jack City, Lash decided to

steer clear of the town. True a sizable fighting force
waited there, but many of the townspeople would side
with the posse. Lash had no wish to be trapped in the
Tumbleweed. So he discarded such money as might be
there. Both he and Reckharts wore bulging money belts
and had sufficient cash about them to keep them in
comfort until things cooled down and they could draw
from one of the bank accounts in which they stashed
their profits.

One question arose. Which direction offered them the
best chance of escape?

Having made a study of the Texas Penal Code, learning every loophole it offered, Reckharts thought of going east, to the more settled areas of the coast. Not so
Lash. The Western-raised man knew that few lawmen
stuck strictly to the letter of the Penal Code, and that no
jury worried unduly over finer points of the law. If he
and Reckharts were to escape, they must go south and
cross the border into Mexico.

"We can go through the cane-brakes, along the trail
Cuellar showed us, and cross the river at Skull
Crossing," he said. "The Texas law can't touch us in
Mexico and we'll head west to New Mexico, come back
over the river when it's safe."

Knowing how little chance he would have alone,
Reckharts fell in with his companion's plans.

While having accompanied Cuellar through the wild
cane-brake country on several occasions, Lash and
Reckharts found going through alone a different prop-
osition. Night found them still tangled in the winding
maze. At dawn, however, it seemed that Reckharts' luck
still held. Coming on to a path, Lash found sign of the
smuggler train's passing and recognized enough of his
surroundings to tell him he could safely follow it. Soon
after the cane-brakes began to thin and changed to
wooded country. Lash figured that he could find his
way easily enough now and that the wooded land held
no danger for them.

He still thought so as the horses swung around a curve in the trail.

"Hello, Reckharts," said a voice.

Two men blocked the trail, standing side by side and facing the riders; one a tall, black-dressed youngster holding a rifle, the other a man Reckharts and Lash both recognized.

Standing looking at the two riders, Ballinger felt cold satisfaction building in him. After leaving Jack City, he and the Kid headed for the cane-brake country by the most direct route. Riding tired horses, they could not make good time and reached that crazy tangle after dark. Unlike Reckharts, Ballinger was guided by a man who knew the cane-brakes like the back of his hand. Following paths with the unerring instinct of his Comanche forefathers, the Kid led Ballinger through to Skull Crossing. A check of the banks told them that Reckharts and Lash had not arrived, so they waited. Now Ballinger knew the time had come to put his lessons into use.

"Move over," Lash ordered. "We're coming through."

"You're going back to Chicago to stand trial for the murder of Patrolman Donovan," Ballinger answered.

"Who's taking us?"

"I am."

"You didn't do so good the last time," Lash pointed out.

"That was last time," Ballinger replied. "Get down from those horses."

Lash studied the two men, estimating his chances. While Ballinger wore a holstered revolver, the weapon sat too high and in a position strange to Western eyes. On the last occasion they had met, the detective had not shown any talent in the use of firearms. The real menace lay with the Indian-dark young Texan who stood on the right. There might be a way—

"You're the law," Lash said, swinging his leg over

the saddle so as to drop down with the horse between him and the Ysabel Kid. "Yeeah!"

Giving the yell, Lash thrust himself clear of his horse and the startled animal leapt forward. The Kid and Ballinger had to jump aside, or be ridden down by the spooked horse. Even as he went, the Kid tried to line his rifle, but the horse hid Lash from him.

Not so Ballinger. The detective started to draw as he flung himself to one side. Out came the Webley an instant after Lash's Remington left leather, but the detective's gun spoke first. Lash had not expected any such reaction and saw the danger a split-second too late. Meaning to cut down on the Kid first, he tried to alter his aim. Ballinger's first bullet caught Lash in the body and the lean man reeled, but did not drop his gun. This time Ballinger did not hesitate. Twice more he squeezed the trigger, ripping home the bullets into Lash's staggering body. The Remington dropped from Lash's hand, then slowly, almost reluctantly it seemed, he crumpled forward to the ground.

Reckharts had moved almost as fast as Lash, but in a different way. Even as his companion started to yell, Reckharts flung himself from his saddle. Not to fight, but in a dive which carried him into the cover at the side of the trail. Once there he started to run, leaving Lash behind without a thought or care.

With both horses between him and the Kid, and having Ballinger fully occupied, Reckharts got clear. He built up a fair start before the Kid could bound across the trail and take after him. The Kid waited only long enough to make sure that Ballinger could handle Lash, then went after Reckharts.

One of the changes Lash brought to Reckharts had been that the Big Man took his share of the work. While Reckharts objected, he worked and found himself far fitter than in his Chicago days. That fitnss stood him well as he ran through the woods, for it kept him ahead of his pursuer. While in something like a panic, one thought repeated itself in Reckharts' head. Once across the river he would be safe from the United States law. With that in mind, he headed towards where he could hear water running.

Suddenly the land fell away before him. Below Skull Crossing, the Rio Grande ran between fairly high banks. The banks here dropped almost twenty foot, but at the bottom lay a wide area of sand which should break his fall and save him from injury.

Desperation gave him courage and he sprang forward, falling down. The sand proved to be soft and he felt himself sinking—and continuing to sink. Too late he realized what had happened. Screeching in terror, he started to struggle, only to increase the speed at which the clinging sands sucked him deeper into their shifting grains.

Reaching the top of the bank, the Kid looked down. Even as he gave the piercing whistle which would bring his horse to him, the Kid knew its arrival would come too late. Without a rope there was nothing he could do.

Following the white stallion as it answered its master's signal, Ballinger ran to where the Kid stood looking down towards the river. A sick feeling hit the detective on seeing no sign of Reckharts. Had the Big Man once more slipped through the hands of the law?

"Where is he?" Ballinger asked.

"Down there."

Looking down, Ballinger saw only the hat Reckharts had been wearing and a convulsively pitching surface of sand. Even while watching, the movement grew less and then ceased.

"What happened?" the detective said.

"He jumped down into a quicksand," the Kid answered flatly. "There's a lot of them on the river."

"Why didn't you shout and warn him?" Ballinger demanded.

The Kid could only think of an old man who had been shot down without a chance and a friendly, hospitable old woman blown to doll-rags by a bomb at Reckharts' orders.

"You know something, Ed," he said. "I never thought of that."